SEÑORITA ETCETERA

ARQUELES VELA

TRANSLATED BY
JULIANNA NEUHOUSER

Also by Arqueles Vela

(In Spanish)

Cuentos del día y de la noche (1945)
La volanda (1956)
El picaflor (1961)
Luzbela (1966)
El intransferible (1977)

Señorita Etcetera

INSERT

PRESS

Los Angeles
2025

Señorita Etcetera
Arqueles Vela
Translation from the Spanish © Julianna Neuhouser, 2025
Introduction © Veka Duncan, 2025

Original Spanish and English translation produced with
permission from the copyright holder, Federico Valle.

Insert Press
ISBN: 978-1-947322-15-8, paperback
ISBN: 978-1-947322-18-9, ebook
Library of Congress: 2024948279

Cover and interior page design by HR Hegnauer Design Studio

Introduction

Veka Duncan

At the outbreak of the Roaring Twenties, a literary figure emerged from the depths of the Maya jungle to become the first avant-garde prose writer in Latin America: Arqueles Vela, his name as mysterious as the man himself. Born in 1899, it is still unclear whether he was born in Guatemala or Mexico. It is said that there is a birth certificate listing his birthplace as Tapachula, in the Mexican state of Chiapas, albeit on the Guatemalan border. Other sources have argued that he was born in Guatemala, among them some of his closest collaborators in Mexico, such as the poet Germán List Arzubide. What we can confirm is that his parents David Vela and Matilde Salvatierra were Guatemalan and that Arqueles eventually crossed the border to Mexico in 1919, as his brother David once confirmed, which means that his childhood and early youth were spent in Central America.

It may seem stubborn to place this much emphasis on his origins, but it's undeniable that it not only continues to puzzle but astonish. One could say that Arqueles Vela came out of nowhere, but it would be more precise to say that it was a place still very much imbued with Indigenous traditions and marked by a rural way of life. That just three years later he was publishing experimental

stories that explored the very definition of modernity is still rather unfathomable. Vela was, however, greatly privileged within the Guatemalan context of his time, which in part explains his openness to new forms of thought and narrative. He was most likely educated at a Jesuit school, an experience that ironically drove him far from religion but nevertheless places him within a certain elite. We also know that his academic background involved studying at a teachers' college. Again, this sheds light on the very diffuse information we have on his early life, as teachers' colleges were associated with the intellectual class and the most cutting-edge ideas in Latin America at the time.

Somewhere along the way, he entered Mexico's literary and artistic circles, where the revolution that had begun in 1910 was still generating shockwaves a decade later, driving a complete transformation of the cultural paradigm. In this process, Vela came across one magazine and one editor in particular that had cultivated the Mexican avant-garde. It was this encounter that shaped *Señorita Etcetera* and the rest of Vela's writings from that moment on.

On October 1, 1920, readers across Mexico came upon an editorial with a rather confessional tone in the pages of *El Universal*, today the longest-running newspaper in Mexico City and at the time one of the most ambitious press ventures of the postrevolutionary period, one that was celebrating its fourth anniversary that day. Written by Carlos Noriega Hope—although signed with his *nom de plume*, Silvestre Bonnard—the short column was originally meant to be self-praise, a moment to rejoice in the achievements of another year, but the director of the

newspaper's cultural supplement, *El Universal Ilustrado*, did quite the opposite.

Noriega Hope had taken the reigns only a few months beforehand, as reported in a brief article published in its opening pages on March 4 that same year. Despite the newspaper's short life, there were nevertheless big shoes to fill at the offices of *El Universal Ilustrado* on Calle Madero. The launch of the supplement in 1917 had been overseen by Carlos González Peña, already a renowned writer and intellectual who had earned his fame in the Ateneo de la Juventud, a movement of high school students that rebelled against the establishment in 1909, marking an important precedent to the revolution the following year. Next in line was the poet Xavier Sorondo, followed by the fascinating María Luisa Ross, the first female reporter at the most important newspaper of Mexico's Belle Époque, *El Imparcial*, who then became the first woman to write for *El Universal*. By the time each of them took over *El Universal Ilustrado*, they were all, in a way, veterans of the written word.

It thus comes as no surprise that Noriega Hope began his 1920 editorial by stating that he did not believe his magazine to be the best, "the princess of magazines" or even a "great" one—probably taking cues from the newspaper's own publicity. The challenges he faced and, above all, the expectations of the audience given the editors that preceded him must have been overwhelming. So, in a moment of striking honesty, he admitted that sometimes readers would find a magnificent issue and one that might seem lazy at others, but he reaffirmed his conviction that he would rather be criticized for putting out an "uneven" magazine than one that was always the same; his goal

was to never imitate others, to always avoid clichés, even the "scissor" of censorship, and to constantly seek to improve the magazine's contents. To achieve this, he said, he brought together the best and most select writers and reporters; astonishingly, none of them were older than 28 at the time (he himself was 24).

Time would prove Carlos Noriega Hope's humility to be unfounded, as his decision to foster young talent turned *El Universal Ilustrado* into not only the most popular magazine of its time—rivalled only by *Excelsior*'s *Revista de Revistas*—but also, and more importantly, the most avant-garde. Although he had inherited some of the most significant representatives of modern literary and artistic movements in Mexico from his predecessors —particularly Salvador Novo and Xavier Villaurrutia, who published their first poems in the magazine in 1919—Noriega Hope soon showed a sharp instinct for selecting those pens—and pencils, lest we forget it was an illustrated publication—that captured the zeitgeist of postrevolutionary Mexico. It's not a coincidence that this transformation from a magazine still somewhat rooted in the styles and aesthetics of late nineteenth century Modernism occurred in the early twenties; Noriega Hope probably understood that the dawn of this new decade also represented a new societal mindset in the wake of the First World War. Under his wing, *El Universal Ilustrado* thus became a place of encounter for the most restless and provocative minds and, more often than not, a battleground for heated debates regarding the path that should be taken by art, literature and humanity itself in this new era dominated by monumental skyscrapers, shiny steel cars and silver screens.

By 1923, Arqueles Vela had joined the ranks of Noriega Hope's young magazine as bureau chief. He was only 24 years old at the time, but soon became one of the primary drivers of *El Universal Ilustrado*'s avant-garde spirit. The previous year he had published his first short story, "Señorita Etcetera," as part of a collection created by Noriega Hope for the magazine called "The Weekly Novella"—which had also serialized Mariano Azuela's *The Underdogs*, still considered the quintessential literary exploration of the Mexican Revolution. With this story, Vela was consecrated as one of the first Latin American writers to embrace the literary innovations of the avant-garde. His second story, "Nobody's Café," soon followed suit, piquing the interest of scholars and critics.

Although the story was officially published in book form in 1926, when Vela had already left Mexico for Europe, its history is inseparable from that of *El Universal Ilustrado*. It was there, in 1924, where he wrote what is generally considered the first draft—for some experts, it could even be considered the first edition—as a short chronicle titled "The Stridentist Afternoon: The History of Nobody's Café." One year later, another text signed by Vela would appear in the magazine with just "Nobody's Café" as the title, the word *novella* in parentheses. Much of what was written in those early rehearsals would be included in the final version.

It's still unclear exactly how Vela and Noriega Hope met, though the latter did explain in an editorial dated April 5, 1923 that the writer had personally given him a chapbook he had written, titled *The Gray Path and Other Poems*, and anxiously waited outside his office in the weeks that followed in the hopes of reading the review

he had been promised. Though it was never published, Noriega Hope offered him a job instead. Vela's star rose at *El Universal Ilustrado* over the course of the decade, not only because he would publish his most important literary work in its pages, but also through his journalistic contributions. Under the pseudonym Silvestre Paradox, for example, he wrote a weekly column titled "As the World Turns" that examined everyday life in Mexico City. As we shall see, a keen sense of observation, particularly regarding social affairs, would be characteristic of Vela's work.

The anecdote of how Vela came to work at *El Universal Ilustrado* suitably accompanied a summary of the day's issue, one that represented a watershed in Mexican media history due to its publication of Manuel Maples Arce's poem "Wireless Telegraphy," which would be read during Mexico's inaugural radio broadcast in May 1923; the station represented a collaboration between *El Universal Ilustrado* and a new company known as La Casa de la Radio. This revealed the influence of Stridentism on the magazine, a movement that could easily be considered to be the only true avant-garde in postrevolutionary Mexico. To many, Vela's presence is a key piece in this puzzle: he fully embraced the movement's ideas and is considered to be one of its leading representatives. It's quite possible that he first came into contact with the Stridentists through their work published by Carlos Noriega Hope. A hint of this can be found in "Nobody's Café," as many of the names of the café's customers listed in the story were also contributors to *El Universal Ilustrado*, some even appearing twice, both under their real name as well as the *nom de plume* they used in the magazine.

Bursting onto the stage in 1921 as Manuel Maples Arce published the movement's first manifesto, the Stridentists called for a total renovation of the arts and of society as a whole in the face of the technological and urban innovations of the time. They also became instantly famous for their irreverence, as reflected in proclamations such as "Death to Father Hidalgo" (considered a national hero for his leadership in the Mexican War of Independence) or "Long Live Turkey Mole!" Beyond their obvious sense of humor, however, the movement's significance lay in their acute observation of the new reality that had taken Mexico—and the world—by storm in the early twenties; they were undoubtedly the first in the country to understand the full scope of what modernity represented. Yet far from being praised, they were marginalized for many decades by the grand narratives of twentieth-century Mexican art and literature, marked by the idealization of rural and Indigenous communities, the Mexican Revolution and communism.

The city, its rapidly increasing pace and the new industrial materials that had taken over its landscape—particularly steel and concrete—became the backdrop to their literary and pictorial work. As their name has it, from *strident* or loud, the noise emanating from this new horizon was their creative fuel. No wonder their fascination for modern machines led them to be utterly enthralled by the radio; to them, there was something almost mystical about soundwaves travelling through the air. Just as Fermín Revueltas painted cables and lampposts, Maples Arce published his poems under titles such as "Inner Scaffolds" or "City" and edited a magazine he named *Irradiador*. He also rode through the streets of

Mexico City's Roma neighborhood on a motorcycle, which he described as the most Stridentist object that had ever existed in an interview published in *El Universal Ilustrado* on September 20, 1923.

The image of Maples Arce cruising around Roma is perfect for understanding the context of "Nobody's Café." The story's title was taken from the name that the Stridentists gave to a very real café that had become their war room, so to speak: Café Europa, located on Roma's primary thoroughfare, Avenida Jalisco, today known as Álvaro Obregón. Just as the isms of turn-of-the-century Europe had converted the cafés of Paris, Vienna and Berlin into breeding grounds for radical thought, Stridentism needed its own headquarters. In his memoirs, Maples Arce confessed that he found the café by chance, ironically on a quest to find a quiet place to read and write in solitude. Taken by the stillness of the café, he turned it into his lair. Born and raised in Veracruz, a state famous for its coffee production, it comes as no surprise that Maples Arce was an avid promotor of café culture in Mexico City. It was not long before there were readings of poetry and manifestos at Café Europa, which in turn inspired paintings like the one by Ramón Alva de la Canal in which the Stridentists are depicted through a cubist lens.

Perhaps this first encounter was serendipitous, but there's something else to take into account with Café Europa. Whereas most Mexican intellectuals and artists were still gathering in the cafés founded in the nineteenth century in Mexico City's then 400-year-old downtown, the Stridentists chose to cut all ties with the past and established themselves in a neighborhood that had been

built entirely in the twentieth century. This decision was quite fitting for the spirit of their movement, which had started out by quoting Filippo Tommaso Marinetti, author of *The Manifesto of Futurism*. The Futurists were probably the European avant-garde movement with which they felt the greatest affinity, as they also called for a complete break with history and academicism, promoting rebelliousness, audacity, speed, electricity and industrial production.

This resistance to continuity did not only spring from the new dynamism of the streets. Much like the experience of artists on the other side of the Atlantic in the wake of the First World War, Vela felt that something had broken in society with the Mexican Revolution and so the country's literary narratives had to change accordingly. He would later describe the seemingly illogical, fragmented narrative of "Señorita Etcétera," with its disjointed images and unfathomable oxymorons, as the product of the chaos caused by the war. Unlike many of his Stridentist peers, Vela's work isn't merely about enthusiastically evoking the thrust of modern Mexico, but also provides social commentary through a profoundly critical perspective. Like the Dadaists, Vela used the absurd to hold up a mirror to the Mexican society of the twenties, which sought to numb the pain of the revolution through silk stockings, radiant shop windows, jazz and flashing lights. "She disassociated in the window of a luxury department store," wrote Vela in "Señorita Etcetera."

Alienation as a side effect of modernity is also present in "Nobody's Café"; this thread running through both stories leads us to suspect that Vela was perhaps not

nearly as excited about the modern city as the rest of the Stridentists. The very name of the café is evocative of the existential crisis that the new city was provoking for many thinkers: the café belongs to nobody because it belongs to everybody, yet each member of that collective everybody is a nobody. Identity has no place in an industrialized metropolis. It seems his characters wander down no clear path, lacking a sense of purpose. Vela's sense of absurdity crushed the dream of the Mexican Revolution, which was already being romanticized as a movement to bring social justice and a better future to all. Art and literature played an important role in legitimizing this narrative, particularly Muralism and the parallel Mexican School of Painting, which advocated for a socially committed aesthetics that would contribute to the country's revolutionary transformation. With social realism dominating the scene, it comes as no surprise that Vela's writings failed to take center stage.

However controversial its reception may have been at the time, Arqueles Vela's *Señorita Etcetera* is a startling read in our contemporary context due to the way in which it connects with our own experiences, making it perhaps more relevant today than it was one hundred years ago.

—Coyoacán, Mexico City, November 2023

Translator's Note

Julianna Neuhouser

"Each person will think what they will of this strange novella," wrote the director of *El Universal Ilustrado* as he introduced the first published story from *Señorita Etcetera,*[1] commonly cited as the first avant-garde prose work in Latin America. "We wash our hands..." And at first glance, the prose of *Señorita Etcetera* indeed appears overwrought—Arqueles Vela undertakes a journey to the outer limits of the Spanish language in his willfully obscure word choices and neologisms, which I have sought to preserve in English. Yet this hostility toward the reader is only apparent: by refusing to allow us any concrete details that could allow us to identify with these stories or empathize with their characters, Vela's abstract imagery provokes the very alienation they experience. Though a "difficult" text, *Señorita Etcetera* remains one of the most rewarding books I know, short enough that

---

1 This collection of stories bore the name *El café de nadie* (*Nobody's Café*) in Spanish when finally published by Ediciones Horizonte in 1926; however, due to the pioneering nature of the story "Señorita Etcetera," we have decided to use it as the basis for the title of the collection in English.

one can revisit it constantly and yet dense enough that each rereading reveals new insights.

"I had nothing left of her but the sensation of a cubist portrait," Vela writes in the volume's final and most important story, and the sensation of untangling the everyday objects hidden under Braque's torrents of angles until they suddenly fall into place is the same one experienced by the reader as they come to understand the situations and experiences contained in Vela's oblique imagery. He captures the romantic torment of Mabelina, the main character of "Nobody's Café," by describing her "brusque hands, uncomprehending their own noisy penury" as her emotions inevitably come to the surface through her unconscious motions, or the "inverse, contradictory thoughts dampening her pupils." Other images are more obscure, such as the "alpinists of elucidating situations" or "her confused silhouette of a sail cutting loose and wrapping around atmospheric masts." Yet rather than being a cold, unapproachable formalist masterwork, *Señorita Etcetera* is playful, even erotic. "The old currents subjected emotion to a scheme, an itinerary, presenting it as a work of architectonic equilibrium, of metalwork, and not as an imaginative, emotional work," Vela wrote in his essay "Stridentism and the Abstractionist Theory." "All that literature is based on an equanimity that life lacks. What's natural and real in life is the absurd. The disjointed. Nobody thinks or feels with perfect continuity... our lives are arbitrary and our brains full of incongruent thoughts." The reader is advised to not get hung up on the literal meaning of any of the images contained in this book, but instead embrace their lack of rationality, which may reveal a deeper emotional truth.

Unlike his peers in the Stridentist movement, who sang songs of revolution after one had already been consummated and wrote paeans to what were then the latest technologies, some of which they even helped inaugurate, Vela's vision was much more ambiguous. "The century's sweating new beauty," as fellow Stridentist Manuel Maples Arce put it in his celebrated Bolshevik super-poem, becomes hostile to the individual in *Señorita Etcetera*, whose characters lose themselves on incandescent streets and are reduced to repeatedly writing their names in order to remind themselves of who they are. Yet this is not an exclusively pessimistic vision: I first had the idea to translate *Señorita Etcetera* many years ago, as I began my own gender transition, and I found myself presenting myself through different names and identities in different contexts given the difficulty of reconstructing a unitary identity under the dominant biopolitical regime, especially for binational individuals who face a double bureaucracy. And so I found myself identifying with the abstracted women found in these pages, marked by their multiplicity, cubist portraits of themselves. I, too, had become a señorita etcetera. Here I think of Allucquére Rosanne "Sandy" Stone's *The War of Desire and Technology at the Close of the Mechanical Age*—though less well known than *The Empire Strikes Back: A Posttranssexual Manifesto*, I find myself more drawn to *The War of Desire and Technology*'s portrait of the breakdown of unitary identity facilitated by first-generation virtual systems: new identities were emerging that were "fragmented, complex, diffracted through the lenses of technology, culture and new technocultural formations...swimming for their lives in the powerful currents of high technology, power structures

XIV .

and market forces beyond their imagination." We can
find an earlier iteration of this fragmentation in Vela's
stories, this time provoked by the modernization and
urbanization process in Latin America.

Such a queer reading of Vela, of course, deeply betrays
the political commitments of the Stridentists themselves,
who were not only known for their machismo but even
incorporated it into their political practice: in *Sovereign
Youth*, the second volume of his memoirs, Manuel Maples
Arce mentions having participated in the Lázaro Cárdenas
administration's campaign against homosexuality in public life. This seems strange to us now, when support for
feminism and queer liberation is taken as a given for the
left and affirmations of masculinity associated with the
right, but this is the result of a post-Stonewall political
alignment: there was a time when support for revolutionary politics was associated with a cult of the virility of the
(inevitably male) revolutionary, a tradition in which the
Stridentists participated and that would continue until the
time of Che Guevara, perhaps dying with him. Though
Señorita Etcetera stands apart from much Stridentist literature in the prominent place given to female characters,
there are still traces of this attitude that ran through the
entire movement—toward the end of "Nobody's Café,"
the two regulars make a series of misogynistic comments,
while the eponymous story includes a brief rant about the
titular character's feminist convictions. The machismo
of these passages would only be intensified in *The Non-
Transferable Man*, Vela's first novel, unpublished for fifty
years, which followed the adventures of his thinly-veiled
alter ego Androsio in a narrative simultaneously more
experimental and misogynistic than *Señorita Etcetera*,

culminating in an assembly of women debating whether or not to declare him persona non grata.

In the story "Nobody's Café," at least, this machismo is balanced out by the sympathetic portrayal of Mabelina's breakdown—"the thousandths of a woman she left behind with each man, which they never exchanged for that thousandth of a man she longed for" remains one of the most succinct descriptions of the bad deal that hetero-sexuality is for women. Rather than attempting to turn Vela's intentions against him, his value as a writer lies in the exploration of these fragments of ourselves we leave behind over the course of our lives: in stripping us of the mask of our *persona*, but not to reveal the hypocrite behind it, but rather the multitude of people we can come to be in different situations and with different people. That we may be fragmentary, but as Schlegel once wrote, each of our selves "complete in itself like a porcupine."

—Roma, Mexico City, October 2023

EL CAFÉ DE NADIE

a Manuel Maples Arce
cómplice en este Café

a Conchita Urquiza
amiga intransferible

NOBODY'S CAFÉ

For Manuel Maples Arce
my accomplice in this Café

For Conchita Urquiza
my non-transferable friend

1

La puerta del Café se abre hacia la avenida más populosa, más tumultuosa de sol. Sin embargo, trasponiendo sus umbrales que están como en el último peldaño de la realidad, parece que se entra al *subway* de los sueños, de las ideaciones.

Cualquier emoción, cualquier sentimiento, se estatiza y se parapeta en su ambiente de ciudad derruida y abandonada, de ciudad asolada por prehistóricas catástrofes de parroquianos incidentales y juerguistas.

Todo se esconde y se patina, en su atmósfera alquimista, de una irrealidad retrospectiva. Las mesas, las sillas, los clientes, están como bajo la neblina del tiempo, encapotados de silencio.

La luz que dilucida la actitud y la indolencia de las cosas surge de los sótanos, del subsuelo de las oscuridades y va levantando las perspectivas, lentamente, con una pesadez de pupilas al amanecer.

En sus gabinetes hay un consuetudinario ruido de crepúsculo o de alba...

Todo está en un perezoso desperazamiento. Las sillas vuelven a su posición ingenua, tal si no hubiese pasado nada, reconstruyendo su impasibilidad y renovando su gran abrazo embaucador.

Los visillos de las ventanas se desprenden de las ensoñaciones que les ha hecho vivir el hipnotismo de la noche,

1

The door of the Café opens onto the most populous avenue, riotous with sun. Nevertheless, upon crossing this
threshold hanging as if from the last rung of reality, one
seems to enter the subway of dreams, ideations.

Any emotion, any sentiment is expropriated and
entrenched in its atmosphere of a ruined, abandoned city,
a city annihilated by prehistoric catastrophes of incidental
regulars and revelers.

Everything takes hiding, skating through its alchemis-
tic atmosphere of retrospective irreality. The tables, the
chairs, the customers are under a temporal fog, cloaked
in silence.

The light that elucidates the attitude and indolence of
things emerges from the basements, the subsoil of obscu-
rities, and slowly elevates perspectives with the heaviness
of pupils at daybreak.

In the booths, there's the consuetudinary noise of
nightfall, or of dawn...

Everything stretches apathetically. The chairs return
to their naïve positions, as if nothing had ever happened,
rebuilding their impassivity and renewing their great
deceptive embrace.

The curtains let go of the reverie that allowed them to
survive the hypnotism of the night and thoughts that are
never revealed fall from the arc lamps.

y los pensamientos que no se exteriorizarán nunca, caen de los voltaicos.

Sus dos parroquianos entran siempre juntos. No se sabe quién entra primero. Van vestidos igualmente de diferente elegancia. Caminan con un gesto de olvido, con la seguridad de que no saldrán jamás de ese laberinto de miradas femeninas, en las que se reflejan como en una galería de espejos.

En su gabinete, se guarecen, el uno en el otro, de la lluvia de las remembranzas...

Sin moverse de su rincón van recorriendo los diversos planos psicológicos del Café, ascendidos por el vaho de los recuerdos, enervados de no haber podido fumarse antes sus emociones.

Han llamado 5, 6, 7, 8 veces al mesero. Un mesero hipotético, innombrable, que cada día es más extraño. Que cada día viene de más lejos, disfrazado del verdadero mesero, políglota, acaso, para no servir sino a estos dos únicos parroquianos que sostienen el establecimiento con no pedir nada. Los demás no se adaptan a su ambiente eterizado de sugerencias arácnidas, desechadoras de cualquier frase importuna de los que franquean su misterio, desconfiados y se alejan temerosos de haber traspuesto la puerta secreta de la vida.

En las encrucijadas cuelgan de las telarañas de silencio, palabras y risas que no ha sacudido todavía el plumero de las nuevas charlas.

De cuando en cuando llega, desde el otro piso ideológico, una ahogada carcajada femenina que, como el JAZZ-BAND, quiebra en los parroquianos las copas y los vasos de su restaurant sentimental.

Las insinuaciones de los anuncios tapizan su ensimismamiento, interrumpiendo su conversación a intervalos

Its two regulars always enter together, the first one in is unknown. They're equally dressed with a differing elegance, walking with a gesture of forgetfulness, a certainty they will never exit that labyrinth of female gazes in which they're reflected as in a hall of mirrors.

In their usual booth, they take shelter in each other from the rain of recollections...

Without moving from their corner, they traverse the many psychological planes of the Café, elevated by the fumes of memories, enervated from having been unable to smoke their emotions.

They've called the waiter over 5, 6, 7, 8 times. A hypothetical waiter, unnamable, ever stranger, every day coming from further off, disguised as the true waiter. A polyglot, perhaps, so as to better serve nobody but the only two regulars who sustain the establishment by never ordering anything. The others never adapt to its etheromaniac ambience of arachnid suggestions, which reject each inopportune phrase from those who suspiciously clear away its mystery, frightfully backing away as if they had passed through life's secret door.

Words and laughter hang from the spiderwebs of silence cluttering its junctures, not yet swept away by the featherduster of new conversations.

From time to time, on some other ideological floor, a muffled feminine cackle shatters the cups and glasses of their inner sentimental restaurant with the brashness of a jazz band.

The insinuations of the advertisements wallpaper over their self-absorption, interrupting their conversation at hanging intervals with the impertinence of those who intervene in table talk without knowing why, driven by

colgados, con esa impertinencia de las personas que intervienen en las pláticas de sobremesa, sin saber por qué, impulsados por un instinto de convivialidad que los hace desmenuzarlo todo, disparatarlo todo:

Ellos sonríen. Sacan de su bolsillo una tabaquera de ideas y encienden simultáneamente, sincrónicamente, sus acostumbrados cigarrillos engargolados de sentimentalidad o rebeldía y se aletargan sobre la *chaise-longue* de sus remembranzas.

Los relojes estacionados comentan las vidas del Café y de los parroquianos enfermos, casi muertos de vivir esa hora inmóvil que retrasa todas las emociones. La hora que despierta de ansiedad el espíritu y lo va regularizando hasta instantear la sensibilidad de las mujeres...

Los parroquianos, subterfugiados de sí mismos, permanecen ocultos bajo la media tinta de sus sensaciones, sospechando la voluptuosidad de la hora estancada, prolongadora de sus lasitudes.

Los gabinetes se abren intermitentemente, desalojando parejas envueltas en la última vaguedad del abrazo que las ha hecho imprescindibles.

Los meseros recogen, con los cepillos de mesa, las migas pulverizadas de impaciencia, las servilletas manchadas de *flirt* y las frases incongruentes, interseccionadas de sonrisas.

a socialization instinct that makes them break everything down, making it all absurd:

They smile, taking a pack of ideas from their pockets and simultaneously, synchronously lighting their customary cigarettes grooved with sentimentality or rebellion as they laze on the chaise-longue of their recollections.

The stopped clocks comment on the lives of the Café and its sickly patrons, nearly dying of living through this immobile hour that slackens all feeling. The hour that anxiously awakens the spirit, regulating it to the point of immanentizing the feminine sensibility...

The regulars, evading themselves, remain hidden under the mezzotint of their sensations, distrusting the voluptuousness of a stagnant hour that prolongs their lassitude.

The booths open up intermittently, dislodging couples enveloped in the final vagueness of the embrace that has made them indispensable.

The waiters take out their table brushes and sweep up pulverized crumbs of impatience, napkins stained with flirtations and incongruous phrases crossed with smiles.

2

Cuando se acercan los dos parroquianos, la puerta se abre sigilosamente, como atendida por el mejor de los camareros. El camarero invisible, silencioso, sin impertinencias, sin atenciones exageradas. Que no arguye ningún argumento orillando a los clientes a ocupar un gabinete determinado o a decidirse por cualquier menú, precisamente por aquel que jamás hubieran escogido.

Al afrontar el postigo, uno de los parroquianos —no se sabe cuál de los dos— adelanta el pie izquierdo, retrocediéndolo inmediatamente con el sentido mecánico de una equivocación subconsciente, cerciorándose de que no es con ese pie con el que debe entrar.

Se le ve ensayar 2, 3 veces, la intención de abordar la puerta del Café, tal si se aferrara a la creencia de que se tropezará, se quedará prendido, atrapado de las argucias de esas portezuelas de golpe, que son los peores cancerberos.

En todo él hay cierta incongruencia de la locomoción, cierta aberración física a ejecutar determinados movimientos que lo enredan y lo amarran, secuestrándolo de todas las distancias.

En la más insignificante de sus actitudes se observa la misma rectificante simultaneidad, la misma insistencia de combinar un movimiento con otro, como si estuviesen ligados entre sí y no hallara la manera de discernirlos. Parece que siempre está resolviendo las claves de su mecanismo.

2

The door stealthily opens when the two regulars approach, as if attended by the finest of hosts. An invisible, silent host, lacking impertinence, exaggerations. Arguing no case as he directs customers to occupy a certain booth or decide on a particular meal, precisely the one they never would've picked.

Facing down the door, one of the regulars—which one is unknown—puts his left foot forward, then immediately pulls it back with a mechanical sense of subconscious error, assuring himself that it's not the one with which one enters.

He rehearses his intention of approaching the door of the Café 2, 3 times, as if clinging to the belief that he will trip and get caught, trapped all of a sudden by the scheming doors, which are always the most fearsome goalkeepers.

There's a certain incongruence to his locomotion, a certain physical aberration when executing particular movements that tangle him up and tie him down, abducting him away from all distances.

In the most insignificant of his attitudes he displays the same rectifying simultaneity, the same insistence on combining one movement with another, as if there was some underlying connection he was unable to discern. It seems he's always solving the puzzle of his mechanism.

Antes de instalarse en un ángulo emotivo, se tropieza consigo mismo y con las miradas de los circunstantes, como si todo contribuyera a desequilibrarle, a impedirle la desenvoltura de sus actitudes.

Al hablar se acomoda en un sitio imaginal, estricto, imprescindible, atornillándose al momento expresivo, con la seguridad de que si se colocara en un lugar equivocado, no podría articular una sola sílaba. Se asegura en las redecillas de la atención que lo circunscribe, previendo que alguna de sus frases lo hará ausentarse de la comprensividad, alejándolo, haciéndolo inencontrable.

Antes de pronunciar la primera palabra se ajusta el traje, se sujeta los botones en los ojales, convencido de que sin esos requisitos se le evadirán las ideas, no podrá encausar sus pensamientos, ni controlar su dinamismo que lo mantiene propulsor, como si lo estuviesen agitando continuamente.

El otro parroquiano está siempre como acabado de caer, con la vaguedad de la línea perpendicular que no ha podido todavía estabilizarse en el punto final de su trayectoria, ladeado sobre sí mismo, como si el destino no lo hubiera balanceado bien.

Tiene el aspecto del traje olvidado en los percheros. La misma flacidez, la misma arrugada indolencia, las mismas características de los trajes colgados, lo animan y lo cuelgan en el perchero de la vida.

Camina con un aire de no haber tocado nunca el suelo y con la ansiedad de querer tocarlo, sentirlo, palparlo y como si de tanto estar suspendido en los tendederos sentimentales, se le hubiese encogido la indumentaria ideológica, lo mismo que a esos trajes que se les deja secar sin colocarles un contrapeso que los mantenga de tamaño natural.

Before getting ensconced at an emotional angle, he stumbles over himself and all the surrounding gazes as if everything was contributing to his lack of equilibrium, confounding the grace of his gestures.

He settles into an imaginary, strict, indispensable site when speaking, screwing himself down at the moment of enunciation, certain he would be unable to articulate a single syllable if found in the wrong place. He checks the nets of attention circumscribing him, anticipating that there will be one phrase that will absent him from understanding, estranging him, making him unapproachable.

He adjusts his suit before pronouncing the first word, securing its buttons in their holes, convinced that his ideas would escape him without these prerequisites, that he would be unable to prosecute his thoughts nor control their dynamism that propels him as if they were constantly agitating him.

The other regular always looks like he's just collapsed, with the vagueness of a perpendicular line yet unable to stabilize itself in the final point of its trajectory, leaning over himself as if destiny had not properly balanced him.

He has the look of a suit forgotten on a hatrack. The same emaciation, the same wrinkled indolence, all the characteristics of a hanging suit animate him and hang him from the rack of life.

He walks with an air of never having touched the ground and the anxious desire to touch it, feel it, probe it. His ideological attire has shrunk as if from being hung out for too long on sentimental clotheslines, like those suits that are put out to dry without a counterweight to keep them at their natural size.

Se sienta en el rincón del Café como en la butaca de favor. La butaca que puede ser reclamada, despojada por cualquiera.

Cuando entra un nuevo parroquiano teme que quiera ocupar, precisamente, ese rincón que le ha deparado la vida.

Está siempre impasible, inquieto, con la preocupación de no esperar a nadie, con la despreocupación de que de un momento a otro, surja el espectador retrasado y reclame ese lugar anónimo, innumerable.

He sits in the corner of the Café as if in a comple-mentary seat. A seat that can be claimed, dispossessed by anyone.

Whenever a new customer enters, he's afraid they'll want to occupy precisely this corner that life has offered up to him.

He's always apathetic, restless, concerned by not wait-ing for anybody, unconcerned that, from one moment to the next, some late spectator will arrive and claim this anonymous, numberless place.

3

En el rincón de su gabinete, los dos parroquianos arrumbados sobre sí mismos, dejan pasar las horas.

La puerta de golpe se abre de vez en cuando, empujada por la resaca de transeúntes.

Es la primera vez que Mabelina entra a este Café.

Sus vivaces, sus perversátiles ojos, llenos de los holgorios de las tardes de verano, revolotean sobre los números de los gabinetes, buscando la cifra exacta, valuadora de sus ecuaciones sentimentales.

$$17 \quad 25 \quad 9 \quad 6 \quad 10 \quad 7 \quad 13$$

—Ocuparemos aquel que debe ser el más acogedor, el más íntimo, el más escondido —dice él— señalando el 18.

—No. Es un número insípido ese.

—Entonces el 15.

—Tampoco.

—¿El 13 que es el predilecto de los supersticiosos...?

—Está demasiado escogido y, sobre todo, muy lleno de predicciones. Aquel que tiene un poco borroso el número. Así no lo sabremos nunca...

—Aquél —dice ella— como queriéndose refugiar anticipadamente en su confidencialidad.

—Está ocupado.

—¿A esta hora? —pregunta Mabelina, sorprendida de que alguien haya tenido el mismo capricho.

3

In the corner of their booth, casting themselves aside, the two regulars let the hours pass by.

The door is blown open from time to time by the riptide of pedestrians.

It's the first time that Mabelina enters the Café.

Her bright, perversatile eyes, full of the delight of summer evenings, skip across the numbered booths, an appraiser of sentimental equations looking for a precise figure.

$$17 \quad 25 \quad 9 \quad 6 \quad 10 \quad 7 \quad 13$$

"We'll take that one, which ought to be the coziest, the most intimate, the most hidden away," says the man, pointing to Booth 18.

"No. That's such an insipid number."

"Number 15, then."

"Not that one, either."

"13, the favorite of the superstitious...?"

"It's too popular and, what's worse, too full of predictions. Let's sit in that one, with the blurry number. That way we'll never know..."

"That one," she says, as if already wanting to take refuge in its confidentiality.

"It's occupied."

—Precisamente, a esta hora en que no viene nadie, es cuando lo apartan esos dos parroquianos.

—Entonces volveremos más tarde.

—¿Por qué hemos de ocupar ese?

Mabelina se queda un momento mirando hacia el gabinete. Después, toma del brazo a su acompañante.

El mesero, absorto, desconcertado, los ve alejarse.

Al salir y trasponer los umbrales de la noche que va cayendo sobre la vagabundez de los transeúntes, con esa lentitud de los globos desinflados, se vuelven a ver, huraños, descompuestos, extrañados de caminar juntos, apoyando la reciprocidad de sus emociones y sus deseos frustrados, a lo largo de la avenida encrucijada de luces.

Las palabras se les quedan en los labios, inhumadas, como si sus pensamientos se hubiesen interceptado de guiones, haciéndolos ininteligibles.

Ante su mirada entrecerrada, las calles se van extendiendo indefinidamente, como si sus pensamientos las fueran alargando.

Sus sombras confundidas y enlazadas se enredan en los ramajes de los árboles, esquemados sobre las aceras untadas de paisaje.

Indiferentes, desconfiados, inexplicables, recostados sobre la incongruencia y abstracción en que se han sumido, dejan caer en el agua de la fuente, sus palabras impronunciables que van dejando círculos de silencio.

Mabelina se yergue, súbitamente.

Él la sigue incomprensible, como sigue a todas las mujeres...

Al entrar, Mabelina que ha franqueado primero los umbrales de su decisión, se adelanta por entre los pasillos intrincados que han dejado los últimos parroquianos.

"At this hour?" asks Mabelina, surprised someone else had the same whim.

"Precisely at this hour when nobody's ever here, it's always reserved by those two regulars."

"We'll come back later, then."

"Why do we have to sit there?"

Mabelina pauses for a moment, staring at the booth. Then she takes her companion by the arm.

The waiter, fascinated and disconcerted, observes them as they walk away.

Upon leaving, crossing the threshold of night falling on the vagabondage of the passersby with the slowness of deflated balloons, they glance back at each other, reserved, dejected, estranged by their joint stride, reinforcing the reciprocity of their emotions and frustrated desires all along the avenue interwoven with lights.

Buried words fail to escape their lips, as if their thoughts had been jammed by dashes, making them unintelligible.

The streets stretch out infinitely before her asquint eyes, as if her thoughts were prolonging them.

Their confused, interwoven shadows catch on tree branches plotted on sidewalks smeared with scenery.

Indifferent, distrustful, inexplicable, leaning back on the incongruity and abstraction in which they're immersed, they let their unpronounceable words fall into the waters of the fountain, leaving behind circles of silence.

Mabelina straightens up all of a sudden.

He follows her, uncomprehending, like he follows all women...

Upon entering, having first cleared the threshold of decision, Mabelina explores the intricate aisles abandoned by the previous diners.

Se queda un momento suspensa, contrariada, anhelante, equívoca, con los ojos fijos en la difusidad del gabinete que hubiera querido ocupar, perdida en la oscuridad del Café que ha doblado sus perspectivas sobre un recogimiento incomprensible.

Llama 5, 6, 7, 8 veces sin percibir, ni siquiera el eco de su voz que se va quedando en los resquicios de silencio en que se han ido escudando los gabinetes, llenos de sospechas y retrecherismos, apáticos, indiferentes, ensimismados, tal si estuviesen rumiando las conversaciones de los clientes.

Contempla el agua de los espejos, encharcada de sombras, putrefacta de lavar tantas veces la coquetería de las mujeres que se asoman a sus confidencias con actitudes desparpajantes.

Sus mejillas se ruborizan levemente, se encienden, avergonzadas de sentirse reflejadas en aquel ambiente sórdido de gritos, de humaredas, de discusiones, de flirteos que ella esperaba se acrecentaran con el desgarbo de la noche que iba adentrándose tumultuosamente en su espíritu.

Asustada de verse entre el desamparo de los gabinetes desocupados, sola, desechada, engañada, levanta las pieles de su abrigo hasta confundirlas con sus cabellos, apretándose, ajustándose toda ella, cerciorándose de que, en realidad se recupera, después de haber disuelto sus pensamientos, sus miradas, después de haber anquilosado sus coqueterías en la frialdad de aquel Café que le descubría la noche impenetrable, en la que se cuajaban todas las pesadumbres.

Se siente separada de todo, refundida entre esa incidencia, próxima a extinguirse en el rescoldo de incendio apagado en que se queda el Café. Presintiendo que la vida se había acabado, que vivía el paréntesis, el descanso de la vida, salió apresuradamente sin tropezarse con aquella mirada que la seguía a través de su incomprensión.

Momentarily stunned, contradicted, wistful, equivo-
cal, her eyes remain fixed on the diffusivity of the booth
she would have liked to occupy, lost in the darkness of
the Café that has folded her perspectives into an incomprehensible withdrawal.

She calls out 5, 6, 7, 8 times without even hearing the
echo of her own voice, which gets stuck in the cracks of
silence shielding booths full of deflection and mistrust,
apathetic, indifferent, self-absorbed, as if ruminating on
the conversations of their customers.

She contemplates the waters of mirrors flooded with
shadows, noxious from always washing up the coquetry of
the women who so audaciously approach their confidences.

She blushes slightly, her cheeks aflame from the shame
of seeing themselves reflected in that sordid environment of shouts and smoke, arguments and flirtations she
expected would only escalate over the coarseness of a
night that was tumultuously taking hold of her spirit.

Frightened by the sight of herself amid the desolation
of the unoccupied booths, alone, rejected, deceived, she
raises her fur collar until it merges with her hair, squeezing
herself tight, adjusting her entire being, assuring herself
that she has, in fact, recovered from having dissolved
her thoughts and gazes, ossified her amorousness in the
coldness of the Café that revealed to her the impenetrable
night in which all her sorrows had coagulated.

She feels disconnected from everything, reforged by
this influence, nearly extinguished in the embers of the
Café's dead flame. With a premonition that her life had
ended, that parenthesis reigned, a sabbatical from life, she
hurried out the door without stumbling over that gaze
following through her incomprehension.

4

A esa hora en que se encienden las luces de todos los gabinetes, los dos parroquianos abandonan el Café.

La puerta se abre, irregularmente. Manos bruscas, desconocedoras de su penuria ruidosa, empujan, atropellan su inmovilidad.

Los meseros, que de día parecen como muertos, se electrizan de pronto, agitando sus somnolencias.

Mabelina entra en el gabinete más cercano, más lejano a su vida.

Como en ninguno puede ser la que es, se indiferentiza, instalándose en cualquiera:

Balbucea lo que él la dijera aquella noche que se conocieron y sonríe, parentizando sus pensamientos con ese murmullo interior que se emulsiona después de la risa, enumerando los subterfugios en que escudaba disimulando su timidez, disfrazándola en una serie de frases y de situaciones que casi siempre lo hacían aparecer como un hombre despreocupado, insolente, intrépido y hasta cínico.

En realidad, lo que a Mabelina le había interesado, era esa manera con que él se excluía de la vida y se olvidaba de todos y de sí mismo, en las calles, en las conversaciones, en los bailes y en las antesalas, con un gesto de no querer inmiscuirse en ningún incidente, en ninguna labor tan complicada y tan molesta como la de hacer el amor a una mujer; en la que hay siempre una espectación y una

4

At the hour the lights come on in all the booths, the two regulars abandon the Café.

The door opens irregularly. Brusque hands, uncomprehending their own noisy penury, overcome its immobility.

The waiters, who seem dead by day, are suddenly electrified, shaking off their somnolence.

Mabelina enters the closest booth, the furthest from her life.

As in none can she be who she is, she indifferently settles into any:

Mumbling to herself what he told her the night they met, she smiles, putting parentheses around her thoughts with the interior murmur that emulsifies after laughter, enumerating the subterfuges shielding him, dissimulating his timidity, disguising it with a series of phrases and situations that nearly always made him seem unworried, insolent, intrepid, even cynical.

In reality, what had interested Mabelina was his manner of excluding himself from life, forgetting both others and himself on the street, in conversations, in dancehalls and foyers, with a gesture of not wanting to involve himself in any incident, any labor so complicated and so bothersome as that of making love to a woman, in which there's always an expectation and an anxiety regarding all the heroics and impossibilities done on her behalf.

ansiedad de que se realicen por ella, todos los heroísmos y todas las inverosimilitudes.

Mabelina, comprendiendo esa pereza de amar que se advertía en sus actitudes despectivas; se había acercado a su timidez, despojada de todos los obstáculos, desprendida de todas las vestiduras espirituales, como queriendo facilitar un pronto acercamiento, como queriendo tonificar esa especie de convalecencia en que vivía y de la que ninguna mujer lograra exhumarlo.

Lo había mirado con la última mirada, le sonreía con la última sonrisa, lo acariciaba con la última caricia. Le daba en el iniciamiento del continuo trato que llevaban, todo eso que las mujeres no dan, sino al final de una aventura. Sin embargo, él no desistía de su actitud arrinconada.

—Yo quiero estar contigo —la decía— detrás de los visillos de su sentimentalismo, como en los sueños.

Mabelina lo miraba sorprendida, incrédula, al principio. Después, escondiéndose en sus abstracciones; bajaba los ojos bajo el sopor del idealismo, entrecerrándolos, alejándolos de los pensamientos inversos y contradictorios que le humedecían las pupilas.

—Te encuentro en todas las encrucijadas sentimentales, situadas más allá de la irrealidad, todavía más lejos.

Ella sonreía, ocultando sus senos, amortajándolos, haciéndolos más pequeños, insignificantes, queriéndose adaptar al irrealismo de la mujer que evocaba.

—Quiero amar en ti eso que no tienes, eso que te falta, eso que te sobra, lo superfluo, para estar enamorado siempre.

Mabelina mientras escuchaba sus frases, sentía impulsos frenéticos de besarlo, de abrazarlo, de exaltarlo. Pero esa actitud indefensa en que él se colocaba en todos

Mabelina, understanding the erotic sloth that could be seen in his scornful attitudes, made overtures to his timidity, cleared of all obstacles, stripped of all spiritual dress, as if wanting to facilitate a precocious approach, offer him a tonic for that strange convalescence from which no woman had managed to exhume him.

She had looked him over with her last gaze, smiled at him with her last smile, caressed him with her last caress. At the initiation of their continuous transaction, she had given him everything that women refuse to give until the end of the adventure. Yet he never desisted in his cornered attitude.

"I want to be with you," he told her, "behind the curtains of sentimentality, as in dreams."

Mabelina looked at him with surprise, incredulity at first. Then, taking shelter in his abstractions, she lowered her eyes with the stupor of idealism, half-closing them, distancing them from the inverse, contradictory thoughts dampening her pupils.

"I find you at all sentimental crossroads, situated beyond irreality, still further out."

She smiled, concealing her breasts, shrouding them, making them smaller, insignificant, wanting to adapt to the irrealism of the woman he was evoking.

"I want to love in you what you don't have, what you're missing, what you have too much of, the super-fluous, so I'll always be in love."

As she listened to these phrases, Mabelina felt a frantic impulse to kiss him, embrace him, praise him. But that defenseless attitude he adopted at all times obliged her to remain still, fearful, as if in the electric chair of love, in a clinic testing the effects and variations of a type of

los instantes, la obligaba a permanecer quieta, miedosa, como en la silla eléctrica del amor, como en una clínica en la que le estuviesen probando los efectos y las variaciones de una especie de rayos ultravioleta que iban descomponiendo su espíritu y sujetando su cuerpo, transmigrándolo a todas las sombras, en las que se contemplaba y se abstraía, reconociendo sus movimientos desmesurados que iban tapizando el gabinete con las decoraciones de los sueños.

Se palpaba en los muros transparentada, distendida, desrealizada por la claridad de sus cerebraciones que la desbarajustaban, la ahogaban de luz, tal si la trasladaran inusitadamente a uno de esos aparadores de artefactos eléctricos en los que todas las cosas se hinchan de luminosidad.

Se alejaban y se encontraban mutuamente en todas las dimensiones, como si a esa luz que los mantenía quietos la hubiese agitado, de pronto, algún viento extraño o la balanceara una idea intermitente. Se abrazaban con esos inconmensurables abrazos que hace la sombra de los abrazos proyectados, de los abrazos que no se dan, quebrados en todas las esquinas de la idealidad, electrocutados por todos los intersticios del gabinete apagado y encendido simultáneamente.

ultraviolet rays that were undoing her spirit and subduing her body, transmigrating it to the universal shadows in which she contemplated and abstracted herself, perceiving her own exaggerated movements as they upholstered the booth with the decor of dreams.

She groped around for the walls, having become transparent, distended, undone by the clarity of the cerebrations disorienting her, drowning her in light, as if she was being uncannily transferred to one of those display windows full of electrical artifacts where everything bursts with luminosity.

They mutually parted and met on all planes, as if the light that was keeping them still had suddenly been agitated by some strange wind, swayed by an intermittent idea. They embraced in one of those incommensurable embraces made of shadows, embraces that are never given, broken on all the corners of ideality, electrocuted by all the interstices of a booth simultaneously darkened and lit.

5

Saliendo del baile, habían tomado un coche. Como él conservara su equilibrio, Mabelina procuraba, también, conservarlo. No sabía si era el vino o las circunvalaciones del vals, pero ellos sentían que las sinuosidades del camino se les iban enredando en los ojos, a medida que el auto aceleraba su marcha.

No hablaban, sino con los residuos de las charlas interferentes que se tienen en los bailes.

—...como baila Ud. tan bien...

—No, pero me gusta mucho el baile...

—...eran la mejor pareja, Ud. y aquel muchacho a quien se le quedaba viendo tan ostensiblemente...

Ella sonrió, dudando y creyendo.

—Es Ud. la compañera ideal en el baile. No se deja llevar de su compañero, sino de los compases de la música.

Volvió a sonreír, confusa, satisfecha.

—Se mueve Ud. como si cada compás la asiera de un ritmo a otro, como si los hilos imperceptibles de la música distribuyeran sus movimientos y los manejaran.

—Bueno. Pero ya nos tratábamos de tú...

—Eso es. Te mueves imantada por la música, atraída por la música. Pareces que presientes los huecos del vals, las evasivas del *fox*, las languidescencias de los *blues*. Te introduces por sus recodos y sales de ellos, al mismo tiempo que las notas. En el *charleston*, juegas a la comba de la música.

5

Leaving the dance, they took a car. As he still kept his balance, Mabelina, too, procured to keep hers. Whether from the wine or the encirclements of the waltz, they felt the sinuosities of the road entangling in their eyes as the automobile accelerated.

They didn't speak but with the residue of the interfering chatter of dancehalls.

"…you dance so well…"

"Not really, but I enjoy it…"

"…you were the best couple, you and that young man you kept staring at so ostentatiously…"

She smiled, doubting and believing.

"You're the ideal dance partner. You don't let yourself be led, instead you get carried away by the rhythm of the music."

Confused, satisfied, she smiled a second time.

"You move as if each beat embedded itself in you from one measure to the next, as if imperceptible threads of music coordinated and controlled your movements."

"Okay, but I thought we were on more familiar terms…"

"That's right. You're magnetized by the music, drawn by the music. You seem to foresee the hollows of the waltz, the evasions of the foxtrot, the languidities of the blues. You step in and out of their curves, in time with

Cuando se baila contigo se tiene la sensación de que se es el juguete automático del trombón, del saxofón, del violín, etc. Los sonidos del violín te adelgazan y te hacen flexible, los del saxofón insuflan y prolongan tu cuerpo infinitesimal, los del trombón te alejan y te acercan, alternativamente, de los brazos de tu compañero.

Mabelina seguía sonriendo, sin saber qué decir, confundida y absorta en las apreciaciones, sin poderse adaptar a los modales del acompañante inesperado que se encontrara en el baile.

—¿Ya es muy tarde o muy temprano?

—Es muy tarde o muy temprano, según...

—¿A dónde vamos? Acuérdate que no puedo llegar tarde.

—A un hotel. En los hoteles siempre es temprano.

—Entonces, mejor al Café de Nadie. ¿Lo conoces?

—No.

—Es encantador. Nunca hay nadie. Nadie lo espía a uno, ni lo molesta.

—Al Café de Nadie, ¿eh?

—¿A dónde?

—¡Ah! Es verdad... Yo le digo. A la derecha.

El coche cambió de dirección. Los árboles, despertados violentamente por la carrera del auto, se iban tropezando a lo largo de la rápida perspectiva.

Comprendiendo que él no se atrevía a iniciar la conversación, Mabelina acercándose, le dijo, casi en la boca:

—Seremos dos buenos amigos.

—A la izquierda, luego a la derecha.

—¿Verdad?

—Indudablemente. No sé a qué viene esa aclaración.

—Por esa manera con que me miras...

the notes. During the Charleston, you skip rope with the music.

"Dancing with you gives the feeling of being the wind-up toy of the trombones, the saxophones, the violins, etc. The sounds of the violins make you seem more slender, increasing your flexibility, the saxophones stretch and insufflate your infinitesimal body, the trombones alternately draw you away and push you into the arms of your partner."

Mabelina kept smiling, not knowing what to say, fascinated and perplexed by his appraisal but unable to adapt to the mannerisms of this unexpected accompanist she had stumbled upon at the dance.

"Is it very late or very early?"

"It's very late or very early, depending..."

"Where are we going? Remember, I can't stay out too late."

"A hotel. At hotels, it's always early."

"Let's go to Nobody's Café instead. Do you know it?"

"No."

"It's charming. Nobody's ever there. There's nobody spying on you, nobody bothering you."

"To Nobody's Café, then?"

"Where?"

"Oh! Right... I'll tell you. To the right."

The car changed course. The trees, violently awakened by the racing automobile, tripped over themselves all along the breathless panorama.

Understanding that he wouldn't risk initiating the conversation, Mabelina leaned in, whispering nearly into his mouth:

"We're going to be two very good friends."

—A la derecha, luego a la derecha. Se para frente a esa puerta del letrero luminoso.

A esas horas, el Café como que se escondía, como que se hacía más inencontrable, más confuso, perdiéndose en la insondable avenida desorbitada de incandescencia.

—El que Ud. quiera —dijo él al camarero—, siendo confortable.

—¿Un reservado para los dos?

—¿Por qué no...?

—No. Imposible.

—Somos dos buenos amigos.

—Sin embargo, tomaremos uno para cada uno. Es lo correcto.

—El 25.

—Bueno. Uno para los dos. Pero acuérdate que soy una señorita.

"Take a left, then a right."

"Aren't we?"

"Undoubtedly. I don't know why you made that clarification."

"Because of the way you're looking at me…"

"Take a right, then another right. Let us off in front of that door with the neon sign."

The Café seemed to hide itself at this hour, as if wanting to become ever more unfindable, more bewildering, losing itself on an impenetrable avenue exaggerated with incandescence.

"Wherever you want," he said to the host, "as long as it's comfortable."

"A booth for two?"

"Why not…?"

"No. Impossible."

"We're two very good friends."

"Nevertheless, we'll sit at separate tables. It's what's correct."

"Number 25."

"Fine. A booth for two. But remember that I'm a lady."

6

—Oiga —dice al maestro, el hombre que acompaña esta vez a Mabelina— haga desalojar a todos del Café. Aquí no hay más parroquiano que yo.

—Señor, cómo quiere Ud. que...

—No me importa. ¡El dueño!... ¡El dueño!

—El dueño... El dueño.

—He dicho: ¡el dueño!

El mesero se retira medroso y presuroso, en busca de alguien que le informe quién es el dueño de este día del Café.

Al regresar al gabinete se asoma por entre las cortinas, tímidamente, balbuceando una lista de excusas.

—En este momento no está.

—Ha salido.

—Cuando regrese.

—Es imposible...

—No está ocupado más que el gabinete del fondo. Pero es como si no lo estuviera. Esos dos parroquianos no hablan, no discuten, no se mueven. Son inservibles. No piden nada. No conocen a nadie. Nadie los conoce.

El hombre irrupto vuelve los ojos hacia el gabinete. No distingue sino las siluetas de dos parroquianos, inmobles, impasibles, pirografiados sobre la media luz que los circunda y los deteriora.

Se queda mirándolos como si no los viera, como si no lograra delimitar sus actitudes inconclusas, como las de

6

"Listen here," Mabelina tells the teacher, the man who has accompanied her on this occasion. "Have them clear out the Café. I want no other customers here but me."

"Sir, how do you expect us to…"

"I don't care. The manager…! The manager!"

"The manager… The manager."

"As I said: the manager!"

The waiter retires swiftly and fearfully, looking for someone to tell him who is in charge of the Café today.

Returning to the booth, he timidly emerges from between the curtains, muttering a list of excuses.

"He's not here right now."

"He's left."

"When he gets back."

"It's impossible…"

"Only the back booth is occupied right now. But it's as if it wasn't. Those two don't speak, don't shout, don't move. They're good for nothing. They order nothing. They know nobody. Nobody knows them."

The intrusive man glances back at the booth. He can't make out more than the silhouettes of the two immobile, impassive regulars, pyrographed against the weak light that encircles them and wears them down.

He stares at them as if he doesn't see them, unable to delimit their inconclusive postures, like those in a frieze,

los frisos, próximos a abandonar, a entrar al Café, apenas agitados por los movimientos inusitados de las cortinas que alargan o encogen sus sombras.

Mabelina se frota los ojos suavemente, como para disolver sus miradas que se han quedado fijas también, fascinadas por la inmovilidad en que permanecen los dos parroquianos, cobijados de mutismo.

Despojando sus ojos de esa ceniza que le dejara el insomnio en los olvidos sentimentales, descotando sus miradas, sus pensamientos, sus sensaciones entornadas por la última mano que la acariciara con una displicente intención de dejarla hermetizada, clausurada, se va desprendiendo del embozo que cubre sus encantos.

—Mira mis piernas para que no te dejes engañar por las de otras mujeres, pruébalas.

Él las besa. Las va palpando, apretando...

—Estúpido.

—Pero si eres una puta.

Las palabras se les quedan, las unas en las otras, trenzadas, confusas.

about to abandon or enter the Café, barely disturbed by the unusual movements of the curtains lengthening and compressing their shadows.

Mabelina softly rubs her eyes as if to dissolve her gaze, which has likewise remained fixed, fascinated by the immobility of the two regulars swaddled in aphonia.

Clearing her eyes of ashes left behind by the insomnia of sentimental forgetfulness, rescinding the prohibition on gazes, thoughts, feelings left half-sealed by the last hand to caress her with the discourteous intention of leaving her hermetic, decommissioned, she lifts the veil concealing her charms.

"Look at my legs, so you won't fall for those of any other woman. Come on, touch them."

He kisses her legs, feels them, squeezing...

"Idiot."

"But you're a whore."

These words get stuck inside each other, interwoven, confused.

7

—¿Eres tú...?

—Casi.

—¿Cómo casi?

—En este momento estoy escribiendo un artículo en el que no hay sino una tercera parte de mis conceptos, de mis ideas. Un artículo que desvía esa trayectoria reincidente de mi manera de ser. Después de escribirlo no sé si, en realidad, sea el mismo de ayer. Soy un individuo que se está renovando siempre. Un individuo al que no podrás estabilizar nunca. Un individuo al que engañarás diariamente conmigo mismo por esa mutabilidad en que vivo.

Cada día besas en mí a un hombre diferente. Un hombre que es uno por la noche y otro con el alba. Canjeas hoy, como canjeaste ayer, como canjearás mañana, a este hombre diverso que parezco hoy, por aquel único que seré después y así, simultáneamente.

En cada noche hay en mí un hombre destruido, un hombre arruinado, un hombre desfalcado, despilfarrado por la cotidianidad. Un hombre nuevo. Por eso, a pesar de tus promesas, no me serás fiel jamás.

—Tú siempre con tus cosas.

—No son cosas. Es la verdad.

—No hagas frases. ¿No quieres mejor besarme?

—Admirable.

7

"Is that you...?"

"Almost."

"What do you mean, almost?"

"Right now I'm writing an article that contains no more than a third of my own concepts and ideas. An article that diverts the recurrent course of my way of being. After writing it, I don't know if I will, in fact, be the same as yesterday. I'm an individual undergoing constant renovation. An individual you'll never be able to stabilize. An individual you'll cheat on with me each day because of that mutability in which I live.

"Each day you kiss a different man. A man who's one person at night and another with the dawn. Today, like yesterday, like tomorrow, you'll trade in this variegated man I seem to be now for that unique man I will come to be and so on, simultaneously.

"Each night I have within me a wreck of a man, a ruined man, a defrauded man, squandered by the quotidian. A new man. And so, no matter what promises you may make, you'll never be faithful to me."

"You're always going on about some old thing."

"It's not some old thing. It's true."

"Don't give speeches. Wouldn't you rather kiss me?"

"Admirable."

Mabelina se convenció, recordando sus charlas con aquel periodista, de que era, en efecto, el único que podía acompañarla desde que se asomara por los subterfugios de la aventura.

Cuando salieron, ya en el coche, él la preguntó:

—¿Por qué has vuelto a pensar en mí?

—Sabes muy bien que eres, entre todos tus compañeros, el predilecto. Los demás son muy indiscretos, muy esculcadores y sobre todo, muy impertinentes. No se les puede decir una frase sin que le busquen, inmediatamente, un sentido transversal. Tú, en cambio, procuras evadirte de lo que se te dice y se te consulta, procuras aligerarlo todo, despistarlo todo, componerlo todo, aunque después lo embrolles y lo descompongas.

—¿Ya no eres amiga de Androsio?

—Me alejé de su amistad por incomprensivo, por equivocado. Una noche fuimos a cenar juntos, luego al teatro, al cabaret. Durante ese tiempo fue preparando sus confidencias, sus deseos y, cuando yo ya me lo esperaba, comenzó a elogiar mi manera de vestir. Con una actitud de modisto o de aparadorista que ha confeccionado la mejor pose de la moda, desató y ató de nuevo el listón que sujetara mis zapatillas, exaltando sucesivamente el color de mis medias, cerciorándose de su calidad. Acariciando mis piernas, me preguntó si usaba las ligas de última moda, con estuche de radio o con el retrato de alguien.

Fue subiendo y aventurando sus caricias subrepticiamente, estremeciéndome, asfixiándome, como si de pronto me hubiesen soltado el duchazo de la voluptuosidad.

Sus caricias eran, en realidad, aquellas que he preferido siempre. Las que más emociones y sensaciones causan. Las que la hacen a una tenderse, arrebujarse, estrujase toda,

Recalling her conversations with the journalist in question, Mabelina convinced herself that, ever since his emergence through the subterfuges of adventure, he was, in effect, the only one who could accompany her.

After they left, he asked her in the car:

"Why did your thoughts once again turn my way?"

"You know perfectly well that, out of all your colleagues, you are my favorite. The others are quite indiscrete, quite intrusive and, above all, quite impertinent. You can't say a single phrase without them immediately trying to find some oblique meaning. You, however, try to avoid all that is said to you and asked of you, you try to lighten everything, sidetrack everything, put everything together, even though you then get all tangled up and everything falls back apart."

"Are you and Androsio no longer friends?"

"I distanced myself from his friendship due to his incomprehension, his misinterpretations. We went out for dinner one evening, then to the theater, then the cabaret. He spent all this time preparing his confidences, his desires, and by the time I had come to expect it, he started praising the way I dressed. With the attitude of a couturier or window dresser that has confected the perfect pose, he untied and retied the ribbons of my slippers before exalting the color of my stockings, assuring himself of their quality. Caressing my legs, he asked if I used the latest garters, with a radio case or someone's portrait.

"His caresses started surreptitiously climbing and exploring, making me tremble, asphyxiating me, as if suddenly caught in a shower of voluptuousness.

"His caresses were, in fact, the sort I've always preferred, arousing the greatest emotions and sensations,

exhausta. Pero al final quería que fuéramos esos pasajeros hipotéticos de los hoteles que regresan de cualquier ciudad, en un tren que no llega nunca, esos pasajeros que no son, sino los turistas del amor.

Tú siempre te quedas en las iniciaciones, en el prólogo, en lo que prefiero. Por eso me tendrás y te tendré en la perennidad de lo improbable.

making you stretch out and get cozy, wringing you dry, leaving you exhausted. But in the end, he wanted us to be those hypothetical passengers in hotel rooms returning from any city on a train that never arrives, those passengers who are nothing but tourists of love.

"You never move past the initiations, the prologue, everything I prefer. And so you'll always have me and I'll always have you in the perenniality of the improbable."

8

Mabelina sentía en los labios el escozor de sus besos. Seguramente él la había visto entrar a este Café y por eso la invitaba.

Apenas si lo conociera. Sin embargo, se acercaba a sus presentimientos, arrinconándose en ese hueco íntimo que le deparaba su jovialidad y sus maneras desenvueltas de hombre acostumbrado a enredarse y desenredarse en las miradas femeninas.

Adivinando una insistencia de entreverla, de descubrirla, de desvestirla, levantaba los brazos con languidez, dejando que sus ojos se aventuraran por los resquicios de su traje.

Presentía sus caricias, las sentía, como una enredadera, ramificándose por todo su cuerpo.

—Nunca creí que te fijaras en mí.

—Yo me fijo en todas las mujeres...

—Como yo, en todos los hombres...

—Pero en todas las mujeres como tú...

Se habían ido acercando, poco a poco, encerrándose en el biombo de sus sonrisas, de sus miradas, hundiéndose en la barahúnda de sus emociones.

Mabelina entrecerraba los ojos como para iniciar esa oscuridad que necesitaban, doblegándose sobre la sorpresa de sus brazos.

Ya en el diván, se fueron llenando de confidencias.

8

Mabelina felt the sting of his kisses on her lips. Surely he had seen her enter the Café and that's why he asked her to come.

She barely knew him. Nevertheless, she endeared herself to her premonitions and settled into that intimate hollow giving him his cheer, the graceful manners of a man accustomed to tangling and untangling himself in the female gaze.

Divining an insistence on discerning her, discovering her, undressing her, she listlessly raised her arms, letting his eyes venture into the chinks in her clothing.

She perceived his caresses, apperceived them as a liana branching out across her body.

"I never thought you'd notice me."

"There's not a woman I don't..."

"Like me, with men..."

"But only women like you..."

They had slowly been getting closer, closing themselves off behind the screen of their smiles, their glances, plunging into the commotion of their emotions.

Mabelina half-closed her eyes as if to inaugurate that darkness they required, submitting to the surprise of his arms.

On the divan, they filled themselves with confidences.

—Te veía mucho, pero tú jamás escuchaste mis deferencias.

—Es que siempre ibas del brazo de cualquiera, al margen de todos.

—Parecías impasible.

—Por mi sensualismo que es puramente intelectual. Las mujeres no me interesan, sino a través de las que hojeo en los magazines. La ropa interior me inquieta más en un magazín que en una mujer.

—¿Entonces yo...?

—Me sorprendes, me entusiasmas, me interesas porque tus piernas son como tomadas de las de esas mujeres que anuncian las medias *Holeproof* y tus senos tienen la misma luminosidad, la misma incandescencia de las lámparas que adornan las grandes salas y parecen hechos del *ice-cream* de la voluptuosidad. Y porque...

—Porque tienes en todos los instantes de tu vida —interrumpió Mabelina— un movimiento retardado para vivir las emociones...

Sus ojos iban apagando las últimas luces del gabinete. De cuando en cuando, se entreabrían pesadamente, despegándose del *Kohol* de sus miradas que la habían ensombrecido, renegrido.

De tarde en tarde, su cuerpo se vivificaba, recordándolo, sintiéndolo y seguía desperezándose con el eco de sus caricias.

"I saw you everywhere, but you never seemed to acknowledge my deference."

"You were always hanging off someone's arm, at the margins of the crowd."

"You seemed so indifferent."

"Because of my sensuality, which is purely intellectual. Women don't interest me except the ones I see paging through a magazine. Lingerie unsettles me more in a magazine than on a woman."

"So, what about me...?"

"You surprise me, you excite me, you interest me because your legs are like those of the women advertising Holeproof stockings and your breasts have the same luminosity, the same incandescence as the lamps that adorn the great dancehalls, seemingly made of the ice cream of voluptuousness. And because..."

"Because, at every instant of your life," interrupted Mabelina, "you have a delay in experiencing your emotions..."

Her eyes turned off the last lights in the booth. From time to time, she half-opened them, heavily, clearing them of the kohl of the gazes shading her, darkening her.

Her body reanimated on odd afternoons, remembering him, sensing him, still stretching out in an echo of his caresses.

9

Al entrar los dos parroquianos, la última frase idiota que se ha quedado flotando en la atmósfera enrarecida del Café, sale despavorida, cohibida, perseguida por los ventiladores intelectuales que lo van limpiando de los resabios de conversaciones.

Los meseros se dan cuenta de que en ese momento surge el alba del Café y empiezan a deshacer, a ordenar la catástrofe de la noche anterior.

Las sillas son desprendidas de sus actitudes pornográficas en que las han dejado los barrenderos, precisamente, después de haberle puesto el gabán al más arraigado cliente, acaso para no dejar que se vaya acumulando en los gabinetes, el lastre inevitable con que anclan los visitantes esporádicos.

Entre todas las sillas hay siempre unas que no quieren desprenderse la una de la otra, que no quieren desistir de su posesión descarada, que se abrazan fuertemente, impidiendo que se les coloque en el lugar estricto, aquel que ocupará el parroquiano consuetudinario.

Los meseros luchan con ellas, como las madrotas con las pupilas que se resisten a abandonar los brazos de ese hombre que no toma nada, que no mira a ninguna de las otras mujeres, que no compra, en esa casa, ni siquiera los cigarrillos y que sin embargo, se le ve todas las noches, como un misionero.

9

When the two regulars enter, the last idiotic phrase left floating in the rarified atmosphere of the Café takes flight, terrified, intimidated, persecuted by the intellectual ventilators that cleanse the air of the aftertaste of conversations.

The waiters realize that dawn has now come to the Café and begin to undo, impose order upon the catastrophe of the night before.

The chairs are detached from the pornographic attitudes in which they had been precisely placed by the busboys after helping the most unmovable customer into his overcoat, perhaps to keep the inevitable ballast that weighs down sporadic visitors from accumulating in the booths.

Among all the chairs, there's always a couple that don't want to detach themselves from each other, that don't wish to desist in this shameless possession, holding each other tight, preventing themselves from being put in their strict place, the one that would be occupied by the consuetudinary customer.

The waiters struggle with them like madams with prostitutes who refuse to abandon the arms of that man who never orders a drink, who never looks at any of the other girls, who never buys anything, not even

Los meseros huyen de aquellas sillas y se dicen recíprocamente:

—Desacomódalas tú.

—Desacomódalas tú.

—Desacomódalas tú.

Hasta que el más reciente, el más encogido —el mesero de los meseros— se acerca buscando el momento estratégico en que estén desprevenidas, para separarlas de la insolencia con que se aferran a su actitud de mujeres viciosas, hiperestésicas, histéricas, atacadas de los peores males.

Las mesas se despistan con nuevos manteles.

Las ventanas se escudan de las curiosidades callejeras con la rigidez de unos visillos limpios.

A todas las cosas se les sacude, se les despoja de los residuos de las noches pasadas para que los parroquianos noveles se sientan satisfechos de haber inaugurado el Café.

En el menú de ayer se escribe:

MENÚ
de hoy

Sopa de ostiones

Huevos al gusto

Asado de ternera

Chilacayotitos en pepián

Ensalada

Frijoles al gusto

Dulce

Té o café

cigarettes, and who nevertheless shows up every night like a missionary.

The waiters flee from these chairs, reciprocally repeating:

"You do it."

"You do it."

"You do it."

Until the last one, the most misshapen—the waiter of waiters—comes over, anticipating the strategic moment to take them by surprise and separate them from their insolent attachment to that attitude of immoral, hyperesthesic, hysterical women, stricken with the worst of vices.

The tables are distracted by new tablecloths.

The windows shield themselves from stray curiosities with the rigidity of clean curtains.

Everything is dusted off, expelling the residue of previous evenings so that newcomers can feel satisfied they have inaugurated the Café.

Yesterday's menu is reinscribed with:

MENU
of the day

Oyster soup

Eggs to order

Grilled veal

Squash in pepián

Salad

Beans to order

Dessert

Tea or coffee

Después de despabilar el ambiente de todos los gabinetes, menos el de aquel que ocupan sistemáticamente los
dos parroquianos, los meseros se retiran a los ángulos de la
espera, resolviendo los problemas de las propinas.

—Somos los únicos habitantes del mundo. Todo
desaparece, todo se muere en este rincón. Somos los
supervivientes de la catástrofe diaria.

—Nuestro Café sería ideal si pudiésemos trasladar a
esta perspectiva la plaza Ajusco, en la que la primavera está
siempre amarrada a sus postes telegráficos.

—En aquella mujer que se nos queda mirando he
encontrado un 50 por ciento de la verdadera mujer que
buscamos, que estamos haciendo en nuestras continuas
charlas. Tan como ninguna.

—Un día, el día del año bisiesto del calendario sentimental nos sorprenderemos de verla, de oírla, transitando
por los pasillos de la introspección, hablando con las palabras que desperdiciamos, que se nos caen, distraídamente,
que se nos escabullen.

—En una está parte de esa mujer y en otra la otra.
Tenemos que presentarlas, ensamblarlas, aunarlas, confundirlas, acostumbrarlas a que vivan una sola vida, con las
mismas emociones, con los mismos gustos. Después de la
amistad preliminar se irán haciendo una, poco a poco. Esa
que será la nuestra.

Hemos inaugurado, hemos puesto de moda a todas las
mujeres...

—Las mujeres no son más que unos aparatos sensuales,
ideológicos, espirituales, sentimentales. Se les puede llenar
como a los acumuladores, de cualquier fuerza, de cualquier tensión.

—Tocándoles esa especie de timbres que son sus senos,
se despiertan en ellas una serie de personalidades que

After brightening up every booth except the one systematically occupied by the two regulars, the waiters retire to the angles of expectation, solving the problem of the tips.

"We're the only people in the world. Everything disappears, everything dies in this corner. We're the survivors of a daily catastrophe."

"Our Café would be ideal if only we could look out on Plaza Ajusco, where spring is always bound to the telegraph poles."

"In that woman staring at us, I've found 50 percent of the true woman we're seeking, the one we're creating through our continuous conversations. Like no other."

"One day, the leap day of the sentimental calendar, we'll be surprised to see her, hear her walking down the aisles of introspection, speaking the words we've scorned, that distractedly fall from our fingers, that slip out on us."

"Part of her is in that woman and part of her is in another. We have to introduce them, unite them, combine them, confuse them, accustom them to living one life, to having the same emotions, the same tastes. After a preliminary friendship, they will slowly become one. And she will be ours.

"We have inaugurated woman, made her fashionable…"

"Woman is nothing but a sensual, ideological, spiritual, sentimental apparatus. One can fill her up with any force, any tension, like an accumulator."

"Ringing the buzzers of her breasts awakens a series of personalities she turns to with the confusion of hotel attendants who don't know if the number lit up on the board is theirs."

acuden con el desconcierto de los sirvientes de los hoteles, sin saber si el número encendido en el cuadro de llamadas es el suyo.

—En las mujeres que frecuentan este Café es imposible hallarla. Sus senos suenan como los timbres de los relojes despertadores, impertinentemente.

—Somos ya casi los dueños del Café. De un momento a otro nos dirán: Bueno. Les parece que cerremos. Están de acuerdo en que se pinten y se decoren de nuevo los gabinetes. Este mes nos han recargado demasiado las contribuciones, etc., etc., etc.

—Es que somos los únicos que comprendemos, que apreciamos su inmovilidad y su alejamiento.

"I've found it impossible with the women who frequent this Café. Their breasts impertinently sound like alarm clocks."

"We've practically become the owners of the Café. Any moment now, they'll tell us, 'Well, it looks like we're closing up. Shall we paint and redecorate the booths? Our taxes were higher than expected this month, etc., etc., etc.'"

"Because we're the only ones who understand, who appreciate its immobility and isolation."

10

Germán List Arzubide, Marco-Aurelio Galindo, Carlos Noriega Hope, Fernando Bolaños Cacho, Oscar Leblanc, Ortega, Fernando Sosa, Otilio Gutiérrez Muñoz, Ernesto García Cabral, Júbilo, José Moreno Ruffo, Humberto Ruiz Sandoval, Manuel Horta, Andrés Audiffred, Jorge S. Duarte, Francisco Zamora, Fígaro, Salvador Gallardo, Germán List Arzubide, Rafael López, Jesús M. González, Santiago R. de la Vega, José Palacios, Samuel Ruiz Cabañas, José D. Frías, Gregorio López y Fuentes, Xavier Sorondo, José Corral Rigan, Francisco Dávalos, Silvestre Paradox, Carlos Samayoa Aguilar, Miguel Ángel Asturias, David Vela, Francisco González Guerrero, Luis Tornel Olvera, Juan de Dios Bojórquez, Francisco Monterde García Icazbalceta, Lázaro y Carlos Lozano García, Rafael Muñoz, Ramón Gómez de la Serna, Luis Amendolla, Francisco Borja Bolado, Kyn-Taniya, Joaquín Carranza, Rafael Vera de Córdova, Luis Marín Loya, Miguel Aguillón Guzmán, Ramón Alba de la Canal, Leopoldo Méndez, Germán List Arzubide, etc., etc., etc.

Mabelina leía y releía esa gran lista y hasta hizo esa salvedad de los cronistas sociales: Y otros que no me fue posible anotarlos, por cómo se iban fugando de la suntuosa noche de fiesta que ha sido mi vida.

10

Germán List Arzubide, Marco-Aurelio Galindo, Carlos Noriega Hope, Fernando Bolaños Cacho, Oscar Leblanc, Ortega, Fernando Sosa, Otilio Gutiérrez Muñoz, Ernesto García Cabral, Júbilo, José Moreno Ruffo, Humberto Ruiz Sandoval, Manuel Horta, Andrés Audiffred, Jorge S. Duarte, Francisco Zamora, Fígaro, Salvador Gallardo, Germán List Arzubide, Rafael López, Jesús M. González, Santiago R. de la Vega, José Palacios, Samuel Ruiz Cabañas, José D. Frías, Gregorio López y Fuentes, Xavier Sorondo, José Corral Rigan, Francisco Dávalos, Silvestre Paradox, Carlos Samayoa Aguilar, Miguel Ángel Asturias, David Vela, Francisco González Guerrero, Luis Tornel Olvera, Juan de Dios Bojórquez, Francisco Monterde García Icazbalceta, Lázaro and Carlos Lozano García, Rafael Muñoz, Ramón Gómez de la Serna, Luis Amendolla, Francisco Borja Bolado, Kyn-Taniya, Joaquín Carranza, Rafael Vera de Córdova, Luis Marín Loya, Miguel Aguillón Guzmán, Ramón Alba de la Canal, Leopoldo Méndez, Germán List Arzubide, etc., etc., etc.

Mabelina read and reread this enormous list, even giving that stipulation of society columnists: And many others I have been unable to name due to the constant comings and goings in this marvelous soirée that has been my life.

Recordando unos, olvidando otros, se esfumaban unos sobre otros, yuxtaponiéndose, formando un nombre impronunciable, indescifrable. El nombre de ese hombre que llegara a ser nadie, de tan ecléctico. El hombre ruso o alemán que fue prolongando el suyo hasta convertirlo en una cadena ecuatorial.

Deletreando las emociones que se quedaran en esa larga lista de comensales que habían asistido a la convivialidad de su vida, iba perdiendo la noción de ella misma.

Se miraba en el espejo, queriendo encontrar en el azogue de los recuerdos, los rasgos que perdiera asomándose a la galería de espejos de la vida.

En todos aquellos instantes dejaba algo de ella. Su sonrisa se había ido ennegreciendo, sus miradas perdidas en las demás miradas ya no eran las mismas que se colgaran de los flirteos, de un extremo a otro de las mesas de los cafés que frecuentara.

Con cada uno de ellos se había sentido una mujer diferente, según su psicología, sus maneras, sus gustos, sus pasiones y ahora apenas si era un *sketch* de sí misma. Le parecía que la habían falsificado, que la habían moldeado, simultáneamente, los brazos de sus aventuras.

La habían ido arrancando una mirada, un beso, una sonrisa, una caricia hasta dejarla exhausta, extinguida, lánguida, derrotada, destartalada, insomne.

De tanto sentir se encontraba insensible. Las voces se le confundían. De sufrir tantos sentimientos vulgares se volvía extraña, adusta.

Después de ser todas las mujeres ya no era nadie. Acaso por esa inconsistencia se encontraba agradablemente en el rincón de este Café, sin nadie, con nadie, como nadie,

Remembering some, forgetting others, they faded together, entering into juxtaposition, forming an unpronounceable, indecipherable name. The name of that man who was so eclectic he would become nobody, some Russian or German man who drew out his name until it became an equatorial chain.

Spelling out the emotions left behind on that long list of diners who had sat in on the conviviality of her life, she started to lose her sense of self.

She stared at her reflection, hoping to find in the quicksilver of memory those traits she lost looking through life's hall of mirrors.

In all those instants, she left something of herself behind. Her smile had darkened, her gaze lost in the eyes of others no longer the one that hung from flirtations from one end to the other of the tables of the cafés she frequented.

She felt a different woman with each of them, in accordance with their psychology, manners, tastes, passions, becoming barely a sketch of herself. She felt simultaneously counterfeited, molded by the arms of her lovers.

They had taken from her a glance, a kiss, a smile, a caress, leaving her exhausted, extinguished, languid, defeated, disarticulated, insomniac.

So much sensation had left her insensitive. Voices confused her. She had turned strange, sullen from suffering so many vulgar sentiments.

After being every woman, she was no longer anybody. Perhaps because of that inconsistency, she agreeably found herself in the corner of the Café, without anybody, with nobody, like nobody, vulnerable to being picked

expuesta a que la tomaran, la canjearan por cualquiera de las mujeres que nadie toma.

Se quedaba, como al principio de su vida, analfabeta de emociones y sensaciones.

Toda ella se había quedado colgada en los guardarropas de los cabarets, hasta con la actitud que le dejaran los *grooms* al colocarla en los intermedios de la noche.

Le era imposible recuperar esa serie de personalidades que hicieron su personalidad.

Los hombres la tomaban equivocadamente, como se toma un abrigo en la incongruencia de una noche de fiesta.

Quería reconstruirse con esas milésimas partes de mujer que dejara en todos los hombres, sin que ellos las canjearan por esa milésima parte de hombre que buscaba.

Se sentía la mujer vaciada, bebida a pequeños sorbos sentimentales.

Había momentos en que se trasplantaba a todos los gabinetes, enraizada en las conversaciones, riendo las frases de los parroquianos, pensando con sus pensamientos.

Se ponía *rouge* para revivir en sus labios el matiz de las caricias prodigadas y *rimmel* en las pestañas para cobijarse en las sombras de sus ensueños.

Se maquillaba con el recuerdo de las caricias como para recobrar sus caracteres fisonómicos.

Apagaba y encendía sus pensamientos con la intención de sorprender en ella ese momento de lucidez y de convalecencia del alba, en el que se pueden reconstruir todas las cosas. Pero no percibía ninguna transfusión luminosa.

Se iba apagando, perdiendo, envolviendo en la difusidad de una especie de insomnio en que vivía.

up, exchanged for any of the women that nobody ever picks up.

As at the beginning of her life, she was left illiterate of emotions and sensations.

Her whole being had been left hanging in the coat check of a cabaret, in the very position the grooms had left her during the night's intermissions.

It was impossible for her to recover that series of personalities that made up her personality.

Men picked her up by mistake, as one picks up another's jacket in the incongruity of a night of celebration.

She wanted to rebuild herself out of the thousandths of a woman she left behind with each man, which they never exchanged for that thousandth of a man she longed for.

She felt emptied out, drunk dry through little sentimental sips.

There were times she transplanted herself from booth to booth, taking root in the conversations of their customers, laughing at their remarks, thinking their thoughts.

She applied rouge to revive the hue of caresses bestowed and mascara to take shelter in the shadows of her illusions.

She made herself up with the memory of caresses as if to recover their physiognomic characteristics.

She flicked her thoughts on and off with the intention of taking herself by surprise in that moment of early morning lucidity and convalescence in which everything can be built anew. But she perceived no such luminous transfusion.

She was fading, wasting away, embracing the diffusivity of that insomnia in which she lived.

MABELINA   Mabelina   Mabelina

M a b e l i n a   M a b e l i n a

Ella seguía escribiendo su nombre sobre la mesa del gabinete, alargando, arrastrando, inconscientemente los caracteres, hasta hacerlos ilegibles.

Las letras se iban extendiendo, horizontalizando, estiradas por el estilógrafo de su pensamiento.

De oírlo tantas veces, de repetirlo, le sonaba a otro nombre. Perdía el sentido de lo que podría significar y tergiversaba su pronunciación.

Lo escribía con la misma vaguedad con que se escribe el nombre de una persona ausente.

Los caracteres, apretados, ligados, se iban tendiendo más y más hasta confundirse con ese horizonte en que se tendían sus rememoraciones.

Relujando sus miradas, se asomaba a cada momento por entre las cortinas del gabinete en espera de su última aventura. La que iba a rehacer o a destruir su vida.

—Hay que gastar, que despilfarrar la vida —se decía— para defraudar a la muerte. Para malversarle sus propósitos. Que nos encuentre exhaustos, muertos, inútiles, inservibles. Que no se lleve de nosotros sino los residuos, lo que no pudimos utilizar, por inutilizable, por desechable.

Sin embargo, pensando esas cosas, sus ojos ensayaban sus mejores miradas, queriendo iluminar los instantes que le quedaran, queriendo comprobar las perspectivas inalcanzables.

No se podía convencer de que sus miradas ya no eran las mismas de entonces, de que habían perdido su acuosidad, de que estaban como desmercurializadas,

MABELINA   Mabelina   Mabelina

M a b e l i n a   M a b e l i n a

She kept writing her name on the table, unconsciously lengthening, dragging the characters until they became illegible.

The letters spread out, becoming horizontal, stretched by the stylograph of her thinking.

Hearing it so often, repeating it, made it sound like a different name. It lost any meaning it could have, its pronunciation twisted.

She wrote it with the same vagueness with which one writes the name of someone absent.

The cramped, connected characters slanted until they merged with that horizon where her recollections reclined.

Polishing her gaze, she kept peeking through the booth's curtains, waiting for her latest lover. The one who would put her life back together or utterly destroy it.

"One has to waste, squander one's life," she told herself, "to cheat death, embezzle its objects. Let it find us exhausted, dead, useless, unusable. Let it take nothing from us but the residue, what we were unable to use, precisely because it was useless, because it was so disposable."

Nevertheless, thinking these things, her eyes tried on their best gazes, wanting to illuminate those moments she had left, wanting to confirm unreachable expectations.

She couldn't convince herself that her gaze was no longer what it was, that it had lost its fluidity, as if

disecadas, filatelizadas, de tanto reflejar los pronósticos de sus sentimientos.

Reía, sonreía y su risa le sonaba a todas las risas. Al escuchar la alegría que se desbordara en los demás gabinetes, iba experimentando una serie de mutabilidades, se iba sintiendo un prolongamiento de cada una de ellas y reía con sus risas, imitando el tono y el efectismo de sus risas.

Recorriendo el gabinete de un extremo a otro de sus recuerdos, se desconcertaba de su manera de andar. Aquella cadencia que estatizara el asombro en las calles y en los bailes, no tenía el movimiento oscilante de los cortinajes agitados, sustraídamente, por los compases de la música.

Sí. Ésta era su voz, pero parecía interceptada por la estática de todas las voces.

En su imaginación guardaba sus actitudes coleccionadas como los trajes de los museos, distinguiéndolos con la etiqueta correspondiente que le fueran colocando los ujieres espirituales de su *boudoir*.

Apoyó 5, 6, 7, 8 veces su ansiedad en el botón eléctrico queriendo llamar a la realidad.

El timbre sonaba, cada vez más lejano, tal si las distancias huyeran y se intrincaran en los cuatro puntos cardinales de lo inalcanzable.

Cerrando cuidadosamente su bolsa de mano, como si quisiera olvidar en ella sus pensamientos, abandonó el gabinete.

Al atravesar los pasillos del Café laberinteados de silencio, volvió sus ojos hacia todas las remembranzas con un gesto de haber dejado arrinconado algo de sí misma en los rincones ensombrecidos, murientes, y de ir a recuperarlo.

demercurialized, desiccated, philatelized from so often having reflected the prognostics of her sentiments.

She laughed, she smiled, and her laugh sounded like every laugh. Hearing the happiness spilling out from the other booths, she experienced a series of mutabilities, feeling the prolongation of each one, laughing along with their laughter, imitating its tone and affect.

Traversing the booth from one end of her memories to another, she was disturbed by her pace. A cadence that expropriated surprise in streets and dancehalls, but lacked the oscillating movement of curtains negatively rustled by musical rhythms.

Yes. It was her voice, but it seemed to be jammed by the static of every voice.

In her imagination, she held on to her collected gestures like museum outfits, distinguishing them with the corresponding labels placed by the spiritual ushers of her boudoir.

Her anxiety pressed the electronic button 5, 6, 7, 8 times, wanting to call on reality.

The bell rang from further off each time, as if distances were in flight, entangling themselves in the four cardinal directions of the unreachable.

Carefully closing her purse, as if wanting to forget her thoughts inside, she left the booth.

Crossing aisles labyrinthed with silence, she glanced back at all her recollections with an expression of having left something of herself behind in the Café's shadowy, moribund corners, and of wanting to go back for it.

The only light that kept sustaining the life of the Café was the one coming from the booth systematically

La única luz que seguía sosteniendo la vida del Café era la del reservado que ocuparan sistemáticamente los dos parroquianos. Al divisarla, Mabelina se queda un momento indecisa. Después, rectificándose, empuja la puerta del Café hacia el alba que va levantando el panorama de la ciudad.

occupied by the two regulars. As she descries it, Mabelina pauses for a moment, indecisive. Then, correcting herself, she opens the door onto the dawn breaking over the sights of the city.

UN CRIMEN PROVISIONAL

A Germán List Arzubide

A PROVISIONAL CRIME

For Germán List Arzubide

1

—¿En qué posición estaba el cadáver cuando usted penetró en el aposento?

—No, señor, yo soy inocente...

—¿Por qué no dio usted aviso inmediato del crimen?

—El señor me dijo que no estaba para nadie...

—¿Desde cuándo conoce usted al interfecto?

—Ayer mismo entré a prestar mis servicios...

El detective hacía estas investigaciones arqueando la ceja derecha como un anzuelo psicológico, y lo hundía en la mirada sumisa de su interlocutor, queriendo desmantelar la sombra del crimen.

—¿Cuántos años lleva usted de servir en esta casa? — preguntó de nuevo el detective al sirviente próximo.

Un silencio prolongado y sospechoso, embrujó el ambiente infestado de preguntas suspicaces y de evasivas comprometedoras, envolviendo a los circunstantes en un capuchón impenetrable de elucubraciones...

—¿Cuántos años lleva usted de servir en esta casa? — interrogó con más entereza el detective.

El sirviente, como si le hubiesen pinchado el timbre de alarma o el botón de su mecanismo, entregó, sin pronunciar una sola palabra, esta tarjeta:

DR. FRANÇOIS BUCHON
de la Facultad de París

1

"What was the position of the body when you penetrated the bedchamber?"

"No, sir, I'm innocent..."

"Why didn't you immediately report the crime?"

"The master told me he couldn't receive anyone..."

"How long have you known the deceased?"

"I only started working here yesterday..."

The detective made these inquiries arching his right eyebrow like a psychological lure he sunk into the submissive gaze of his interlocutor, seeking to dismantle the shadow of the crime.

"For how many years have you been serving in this house?" the detective asked the next servant.

A prolonged, suspicious silence bewitched this atmosphere infested with skeptical questions and compromising evasions, enveloping those present in an impenetrable cowl of lucubrations...

"For how many years have you been serving in this house?" the detective asked again, more firmly.

As if someone had pricked the alarm bell or the button of his mechanism, the servant handed him a card without pronouncing a single word:

DR. FRANÇOIS BUCHON
of the Faculty of Paris

—¿Esto qué significa y qué aclara? —inquirió violento el detective.

El sirviente persistía en su actitud idéntica, contemplándolo con una mirada ausente.

—Conteste usted, explíquese...

El ujier interrogado con anterioridad balbuceó unas cuantas sílabas, ininteligibles por la brusca interrupción del detective que, llevándose a los labios el bastón complicado como una varita mágica, le imponía callar.

—¡Conteste usted. Explíquese. O se le considerará culpable! —insistió el detective, queriendo remover con el remolino de sus interrogaciones, los pensamientos de aquel hombre petrificado de ignorancia, sostenido, únicamente por la "plomada" de la estupefacción, que lo hacía conservar un equilibrio infinito...

—El ujier es... —observó de nuevo el otro sirviente.

—¡Cállese! ¿Por qué no habló cuando fue interrogado? —volvió a objetar el detective—. En estos momentos no se le pregunta nada.

Y dirigiéndose al sirviente que permanecía impasible:
—Su manera de proceder lo perjudica. ¡Hable!

El ujier, con una solemnidad de las noches de recepción, entregó una segunda tarjeta:

FERDINAND ROSSNERBACH
Ingeniero de minas

La situación se iba haciendo insoportable. Frenético el detective, casi ahogándose y tambaleándose de sinrazón, salvó la distancia hasta encararse con su interlocutor y, con un ademán decidido, desde la encrucijada de las sospechas, colocó el revólver en la sien del ujier amenazándole estentóreamente.

"What's the meaning of this? And what does it tell us?" the detective violently inquired.

The servant persisted in his selfsame attitude, contemplating him with an absent gaze.

"Answer me, explain yourself…"

The footman who had been questioned first stuttered a few syllables, unintelligible under the brusque interruption of the detective, who imposed silence by raising an overwrought cane to his lips like a magic wand.

"Answer me. Explain yourself. Or you'll be considered guilty!" insisted the detective, hoping his whirlwind interrogation would clear away the thoughts of a man petrified from ignorance, kept upright only by the plumb bob of stupefaction that allowed him to conserve his infinite equilibrium…

The other servant spoke up again: "The footman is…"

"Quiet! Why didn't you have anything to say when you were being questioned?" the detective objected. "You are being asked nothing at this time."

And addressing the one who remained impassive: "Your actions do nothing but prejudice you. Speak!"

With a solemnity of reception nights, the footman handed him a second card:

FERDINAND ROSSNERBACH
Mining Engineer

The situation was becoming unbearable. Frenzied, almost drowning and swaying with unreason, the detective closed the remaining distance to confront his interlocutor and decisively placed his revolver against the footman's temple, threatening him stentoriously from the crossroads of suspicion.

—¡Declare usted...! ¡O disparo!...

El sirviente, untado del *make-up* de la sorpresa y del miedo, en esos instantes llenos de incongruencia, de los que no veía la manera de salir, con una temblorosa decisión, entregó la tercera tarjeta:

ARCADY KOPEIKEVITCH KALKACHOV
Embajador

Y rectificando la fisonomía del detective, temiendo haberse equivocado de tarjeta, examinó detenidamente la mirada "eclatante" de su amenazador, lo comparó con la fotografía mental que le habían grabado las instrucciones de su amo y, con un gesto adivinatorio, decidió canjearla por esta otra:

RICHARD BAXTER
Abogado y notario

Conservando la impresión de haber encontrado, al fin, después de tantos ensayos, al verdadero individuo que esperaba.

—¡Prendedlo! —ordenó el detective, guardándose el revólver. Y disponiéndose a practicar un reconocimiento minucioso, abrió los cajones del escritorio americano, logrando descubrir los resortes secretos que lo escudaban de la curiosidad doméstica. Cartas en inglés, en francés, en italiano, en alemán, en checoeslovaco, en ruso, en persa, etc. Retratos de artistas dedicados confidencialmente... Claves telegráficas, guías de ferrocarriles trascontinentales, papel timbrado con iniciales diferentes... Pero nada que orientara las investigaciones por un camino seguro.

"Make your statement…! Or I'll shoot…!"

The servant, painted with the makeup of surprise and fear in those instants full of incongruity from which he saw no escape, handed him a third card with trembling resolve:

ARCADY KOPEIKEVITCH KALKACHOV
Ambassador

And challenging the detective's physiognomy, fearing he had confused the cards, he carefully examined his intimidator's withering gaze, compared it with the mental photograph upon which his master's instructions were engraved and, with a prophetic gesture, decided to exchange it with another:

RICHARD BAXTER
Lawyer and Notary Public

While maintaining the impression of having finally found, after so many rehearsals, the true individual he was looking for.

"Arrest him!" ordered the detective, holstering his revolver. And preparing to conduct a meticulous inspection, he opened the drawers of the rolltop desk, managing to discover the secret mechanisms that shielded it from domestic curiosity. Letters in English, French, Italian, German, Czechoslovak, Russian, Persian, etc. Confidentially dedicated portraits of artists… Telegraphic codebooks, transcontinental railway guides, stationary with varying letterheads… But nothing that would guide the investigation down a sure path.

2

Sobre el diván, la muerta tenía el aspecto y las características de los accidentes provocados por la subconstancia...

Ninguna violencia, ninguna presión la había hecho
reclinarse al borde de las vicisitudes. En los pliegues de
su traje, se transparentaba una actitud conforme y hasta
cierto coincidente desparpajo, tal si se hubiese puesto de
acuerdo para finalizar el crimen.

Parecía que la muerta había sido afocada en una pose
escogida por ella misma...

Todas las apariencias de un crimen se perdían ante la
posición en que quedara el cadáver después de la presunta
tragedia que reconstruía su inmovilidad.

Los labios, con el último *rouge* de la coquetería, se
entreabrían, subrayando las frases qué indudablemente,
obligaron al criminal a tomar una determinación radical
y despistadora.

El crimen se cometió sin premeditación, sin alevosía y
sin ventaja... Era un crimen hipotético...

Las manos se quedaron orientadas hacia los puntos
cardinales de los acontecimientos, como las aspas de un
molino, marcando la dirección del viento infausto que las
desgonzara...

El cadáver esmaltado de una vividez epidérmica, tal
si hubiese sufrido solamente un cambio atmosférico,
retenía y se aferraba a la tranquilidad en que la sorprendió
el criminal. Las facciones se esfumaron un poco y, sin

2

On the divan, the dead woman had the appearance and characteristics of those accidents caused by underconstancy…

No violence, no pressure had made her lean back on the verge of vicissitudes. The creases of her dress revealed a conformist attitude and even a certain coincident impudence, as if she had agreed to the finalization of the crime.

It seemed the dead woman had been framed in a pose she had chosen herself…

All signs of crime were lost in the position in which the body had been left following the alleged tragedy that rebuilt her immobility.

Lips red with the final rouge of coquetry opened slightly, underlining the phrases that undoubtedly obligated the criminal to take such a radical, deceitful decision.

The crime was committed without premeditation, without malice and without motive… It was a hypothetical crime…

Her hands were oriented toward the cardinal directions of the events, like the blades of a mill marking the current of the fateful wind unhinging them…

This body enameled with an epidermic vividness, as if it had only suffered an atmospheric change, retained and clung to the tranquility in which the criminal had taken her by surprise. Her features had faded slightly and yet her seamless, incomparable beauty nevertheless persisted.

embargo, persistía una belleza inconsútil e incomparable. Su semblante daba la sensación de que, en el momento instantáneo de la muerte, se insufló de los atractivos que la hicieron encantadora.

Se quedó olvidada en aquella actitud con la que conquistara más miradas... En una pose de la muerte... Por esa irrealidad, los médicos legistas que practicaron el reconocimiento, se consideraron incompetentes para rendir un informe satisfactorio y dilucidante. Habían fracasado en sus observaciones científicas y confesaban su incompetencia, analizando las causas que produjeron una muerte semejante, tan llena de las claridades de la vida. Sin duda, era una muerte de salón...

La frialdad y la rigidez de la suave languidescencia con que se recostó sobre su desgracia premeditada, eran las únicas pruebas del crimen.

Al principio, los médicos creyeron en un intoxicamiento involuntario, de esos que se registran frecuentemente en las reuniones elegantes, en las citas furtivas o en las expansiones de los sentidos...

La complicidad de esta mujer en el asesinato era innegable, por la apariencia que tenía de haber muerto en un *flirt* del suicidio...

Presentaba matices de una muerte de ensueño, de una envenenada de emociones... Su letargo era el mismo de las mujeres que se desmayan en los recodos de las pesadillas...

Una muerte etérea, provocada por un descuido agradable e incomprensible, la cubría, tal si hubiesen tendido sobre ella un velo de condescendencia.

Todo se embrollaba y todo se iba haciendo inexplicable. Los médicos no encontraron y no reconocieron sino la huella de una caricia sutil que había contuccionado la gracia de su cuerpo y sacudido la alegría de su sonrisa...

Her semblance gave the sensation that, in the instantaneous moment of death, she had been insufflated with the charms that made her so delightful.

She had been left forgotten in that attitude she had used to conquer the gazes of others... In a death pose... Because of that irreality, the doctors conducting the examination declared themselves unable to deliver a satisfactory, explanatory report. They had failed in their scientific observations and confessed their incompetence at analyzing the causes of such a death, so full of the clairvoyalities of life. It was doubtlessly a salon death...

The coldness and rigidity of the soft languidity in which she lay back on her premeditated disgrace constituted the only evidence of the crime.

At first, the doctors believed it to be an involuntary intoxication, those that frequently occur at elegant parties, clandestine rendezvous or expansions of the senses...

The woman's complicity in the murder was undeniable in light of the appearance that she had died in a suicidal flirtation...

There were the shades of a fatal reverie, a poisoning of emotions... Her lethargy that of women who faint in the crooks of nightmares...

An ethereal death, provoked by a pleasant, incomprehensible oversight, shrouded her body as if a veil of condescension had been stretched out over her.

Everything was getting entangled, becoming inexplicable. The doctors didn't find and didn't recognize anything but the mark of a subtle caress that had contuctioned the grace of her body and shaken the happiness of her smile...

3

—Este crimen —dijo el detective—, no está en el catálogo de mis observaciones. Parece que fue cometido por un hipnotista o por un prestidigitador. Acaso éste sea el mismo de las tarjetas...

El revólver indudablemente lo disparó una mano espiritualista. La actitud de la asesinada es idéntica a la de esas mujeres que duermen en los escenarios en un acto de ilusionismo...

El arma que le quitó la vida no es un arma cualquiera... Parece que una corriente eléctrica la hubiese desencajado...

Un revólver eléctrico de esos de última invención...

El asesino es, seguramente, un inventor...

La tragedia ocurrió en un salón que no es éste...

La víctima fue trasladada al diván, después de haberse cometido el crimen, de otra manera no se explica que haya quedado recostada tan delicadamente...

El cadáver da la sensación de que ha sido colocado por una mano cuidadosa y amiga, una mano perspicaz y conocedora de los encantos femeninos... Entonces el asesino no es el de las tarjetas...

La única violencia observable es la de sus piernas que tienen una actitud mecánica, como si las hubieran cruzado después de la refrigeración de la muerte...

Tras esas reflexiones, el detective se quedó un momento pensativo, contemplando sagazmente el decorado oriental

3

"This crime," said the detective, "can't be found in my catalog of observations. It seems to have been committed by a hypnotist or a conjurer. Perhaps the very man with the cards...

"The revolver was doubtlessly fired by a spiritualist hand. The position of the victim is identical to that of women who fall asleep onstage during illusionist performances...

"The weapon that took her life wasn't just any weapon... It seems an electric current undid her...

"The latest model of electric revolver...

"The murderer must surely be an inventor...

"The tragedy occurred in some other salon...

"The victim was moved to the divan after the crime was committed, there's no other explanation for such delicate positioning...

"The corpse suggests it was arranged by a careful, amicable hand, a discerning hand familiar with feminine charms... The murderer is therefore not the man with the cards...

"The only observable violence is the mechanical attitude of her legs, as if they had only been crossed after the refrigeration of death..."

Following these reflections, the detective paused for a moment, pensive, sagely contemplating the oriental

de la alfombra, la pesadumbre del mobiliario, los cortinajes suntuosos de la habitación, queriendo percibir el rumor de los pasos del criminal y buscando el botón del *chaqué* que siempre se queda sobre un edredón, como un punto muerto de las pesquisas...

Ninguna mancha de sangre. Ningún indicio de luchas. Ninguna puerta forzada. Los picaportes funcionaban estrictamente, aceitados por la probable pasividad que había reinado siempre en esa casa, tal vez hasta en los momentos precisos del crimen.

Todo parecía increíble en este asesinato lleno de erratas que desconcertaban las meditaciones del detective.

Empezó a recorrer lentamente las habitaciones, deteniéndose, de cuando en cuando, en los ángulos que iban haciendo sus pensamientos en el convergentismo de las investigaciones.

Descorrió las persianas y los visillos de los ventanales. Una claridad exacerbante tapizo las paredes del salón circunspecto.

Apagó sus pensamientos aguzando los oídos, cerrando los ojos como para reconstruir mejor las escenas que se sucedieran tras las bambalinas improvisadas de los cortinajes, queriendo escuchar el eco de las frases comprometedoras que, a veces, se quedan enredadas en las resonancias de las habitaciones asfixiantes de soledad...

Encendió su linterna sorda para seguir, entre tanta despistadora claridad, paso a paso, los movimientos del asesino, estampados en la alfombra, y fue marcando, personalmente, la trayectoria de las pisadas criminales...

design of the rug, the heaviness of the furniture, the room's lush curtains, wanting to perceive the rumor of criminal footsteps and seeking out the waistcoat button that's always left lying on the duvet, like a dead point of the inquest...

No bloodstains. No signs of a struggle. No forced entry. The latches functioned rigorously, oiled by the likely laxity that had always reigned in this house, perhaps even in the precise moment of the crime.

Everything seemed incredible in this murder brimming with errata that unsettled the detective's meditations.

He slowly began inspecting each room, stopping from time to time in the angles being created by his thoughts in the convergentism of investigations.

He drew back the blinds and drapes from the picture windows. An aggravating clarity papered the walls of the circumspect salon.

He turned off his thoughts, pricking his ears and closing his eyes as if to better reconstruct the scenes enacted behind this improvised drop curtain, hoping to hear the echo of the compromising phrases occasionally entangled in the resonances of rooms asphyxiating with loneliness...

He lit his deaf lantern to follow, through so much misleading clarity, each step of the killer's movements stamped upon the rug, personally marking the trajectory of those criminal tracks...

4

El gesto hosco del detective, cambió instantáneamente. Se aclararon sus pensamientos y se entreabrió una maliciosa sonrisa en sus labios exhaustos de preguntas...

La escalinata rechinó bajo la cadencia de unas pisadas femeninas acompasadas y puntuales. En el reloj sonaron, alternativamente, con los pasos armónicos y alegres, 10 o 12 campanadas...

El ruido de unas puertas que se desperezaban como unos brazos después de grandes noches aletargadas, estatizó su mirada buceante.

El pestañeo del detective coincidió hacia un mismo punto y parecía que una idea persistente horadaba sus preocupaciones.

Manos acostumbradas a este ajetreo, trasegaban papeles. El plumero sacudía la pereza de las cosas...

El detective siguió con la imaginación los ruidos que se sucedieron simultáneamente, esperando escuchar un ruido falso, denunciador. Un indicio. Una revelación. Pero todo era matemático y natural. Todo indicaba que esos ruidos eran los ruidos de siempre, los ruidos que hacían la música diaria en aquella habitación.

Las pisadas cadenciosas volvieron a interrumpir la quietud molesta que lo aprisionaba. Iba y venía de un rincón a otro del silencio en que estaban sumidos todos.

Los pasos se fueron oyendo, cada vez más cercanos.

4

The detective's sullen expression transformed in an instant. His thoughts fell into place and a malicious smile broke across lips exhausted from questioning...

The staircase creaked under the cadence of feminine steps, punctual and metrical. Alternating with these harmonic, happy footfalls, the clock tolled 10 or 12 times...

The noise of doors stretching out like arms after long, lethargic nights expropriated his submerged gaze.

The detective's blinking coincided toward a like point and it seemed a persistent idea pierced his preoccupations.

Hands accustomed to such bustle shuffled papers. The featherduster swept away the laziness of things...

The detective followed these simultaneous noises through his imagination, waiting for a false, telltale noise. A clue. A revelation. But everything was mathematical and natural. Everything indicated that these noises were the same noises as always, the noises that made up the room's daily music.

The cadential steps once again interrupted the unpleasant quietude that imprisoned him, coming and going from one corner to another of the silence in which they were all immersed.

The steps could be heard coming ever closer.

From time to time, they came right up to the threshold of the door, the one waiting to be opened under the

De cuando en cuando, llegaban hasta el umbral de la puerta, esa que esperaba se abriera bajo el impulso de unas manos comprometidas. Acaso éstas que alborotaran los papeles buscando la carta denunciadora, tal vez ya quemada en estos instantes...

Los pasos se acercaban y se presentía que, de un momento a otro, sonarían en medio de la espectación. Pero se alejaron temiendo pisar el lugar del crimen, despavoridos de encontrarse con algo inusitado.

Las miradas y los pensamientos del detective cambiaron de ruta. Se levantó del sillón en que meditaba y fue caminando, poco a poco, hacia la puerta en que se estacionaron los pasos...

La abrió de un golpe y su mirada acechadora desconcertó la de una mujer alta, morena, de grandes ojos selváticos, vestida de elegancias, con actitudes de haber vivido una tercera parte de su vida.

Se quedaron estáticos, contemplándose largos instantes, queriéndose descubrir el uno al otro, queriéndose explicar el repentino encuentro...

Ella sonrió ligera y fácil, con esa sonrisa que tienen las mujeres para cualquier aventura, para cualquier sorpresa...

El detective continuó diseccionándola, auscultándola y con una gran cortesía le tendió la mano...

Caminaron unos cuantos pasos y volvieron a verse casi camaradilmente.

—¿Qué hacía usted? ¿Qué buscaba usted, con tanta actividad? —preguntó el detective—, sonriendo con suspicacia.

—Quería cerciorarme de la habitación preferida por él, este día.

—¿Quién es él?

impulse of compromised hands. Perhaps the same hands that had unsettled those papers looking for the telltale letter, likely already being burnt...

The steps approached and it felt that, from one moment to the next, they would resound in the midst of expectation. But then they wandered off, afraid to set foot in the crime scene, terrified of coming across something unusual.

The detective's gaze and thoughts changed direction. He got up from the armchair where he had been meditating and started walking slowly toward the door those feet had parked behind...

He pushed open the door and his tenacious gaze disturbed that of a tall, elegantly dressed, dark-skinned woman with enormous, untamed eyes that had seemingly already seen a third of what they would see in life.

They were left in stasis, contemplating each other for lengthy instants, each wanting to discover the other, explain this sudden encounter...

She smiled lightly and easily, with that smile women use for any adventure, any surprise...

The detective continued dissecting her, auscultating her, courteously offering her his hand...

They advanced a few steps before giving each other an almost comradely glance.

"What were you doing? What were you so energetically seeking?" asked the detective, smiling with mistrust.

"I wanted to see which room he'll prefer today."

"Who is he?"

"Precisely today, I don't know what to call him. Yesterday he presented himself as François Buchon, a doctor from the Faculty of Paris... At other times he

—Precisamente hoy, no sé cómo se llame. Ayer se presentó como François Buchon, médico de la Facultad de París... Otras veces se hace pasar por Ferdinand Rossnerbach, ingeniero de minas, y otras, por Richard Baxter, abogado y notario... ¿Es usted el negociante que tenía que verlo?...

—¿Negociante?... ¿Negociante?... ¡No!...

—¿Entonces, por qué me tomó usted del brazo como si ya estuviésemos presentados?

—Por intuición y porque es usted la mujer que esperaba.

Ella sonrió. Sus cabellos sedosos de caricias, se alborotaron con los movimientos de su cabeza ladeada hacía el almohadón de la coquetería... Y con un gesto insinuante, preguntó:

—¿Yo la mujer... que usted...? —Y, sin poderse contener desgajó una carcajada afirmativa y dudosa.

—Sí, usted es la mujer que esperaba. No se asombre. Confiese usted lo que sabe.

—Es un hombre muy raro... Me paga un sueldo inmerecido, únicamente porque atienda con gracia a los que lo visitan... Y por copiar en varios idiomas, cartas que no sé a dónde van...

Unas veces es un hombre distinguido, elegante, guapo, que mira a través de su monóculo con una mirada insostenible y conquistadora... Otras, es un individuo cualquiera, despreocupado, con lentes gruesos como de sabio... con barba descuidada y cabellera canosa... Otras, un hombre de salón, frívolo y atractivo, rasurado completamente y peinado con *stacomb*... Hay semanas que no sale de su recibidor particular y otras que no se le ve ni un momento. Llega siempre en un coche de marca diferente.

passes as the mining engineer Ferdinand Rossnerbach, still others as Richard Baxter, lawyer and notary public... Are you the businessman who had been wanting to see him...?"

"Businessman...? Businessman...? No...!"

"So why did you take me by the arm as if we had already been introduced?"

"Intuition, and because you're the woman I've been waiting for."

She smiled. The movements of her head disheveled hair silky from caresses as she leaned toward the pillow-case of coquetry... And with an insinuating gesture, she asked:

"I'm the woman... that you...?" Unable to hold herself back, she broke off an affirmative, doubtful cackle.

"Yes, you're the woman I've been waiting for. Don't act surprised. Confess what you know."

"He's a very strange man... He pays me a salary I don't deserve simply because I gracefully receive all his guests... And for copying letters in various languages that are sent off to who knows where...

"Sometimes he's a distinguished, elegant, handsome man who stares an unsustainable, conquering stare through his monocle... At others, he's just another individual, indifferent, with thick glasses like a sage... an untrimmed beard and gray hair... Still others, he's a creature of salons, frivolous and attractive, freshly shaved, his hair styled with Stacomb... There are weeks he never leaves his private antechamber and others he's never even seen at all. He always arrives in a different model of car.

"He receives a spiritless lady in the darkened salon and one with violet circles under her eyes in the salon

En el salón oscuro recibe a una dama lánguida y en el salón que nunca he podido ver, a una de ojeras violáceas. Lo busca mucha gente. Sobre todo mujeres. Su vida es un misterio. Yo no sé, hasta ahora, por qué entran y salen tantas personas de esta casa. Unas vuelven. A otras ni siquiera se les recuerda...

—¿Cómo entró usted a esta casa?...

—Leyendo un AVISO OPORTUNO... Ese que dice:

"Muchacha bonita, discreta, se necesita. —Despacho particular. —Buen sueldo. —Tel. 123-12."

Nos presentamos toda una colección y, entre las más prometedoras, yo fui la elegida...

—¿Conoce usted sus gustos femeninos?...

—Son muchos y desiguales... En su recibidor secreto, guarda una panoplia de miradas y de sonrisas...

Tiene predilección por las muertas... O por las que se mueren y le dejan una sensación, una emoción última, incontinuable, "irrepresible", que no podrá obtener nadie, que no podrá saborear nadie... O por las que hacen como que se mueren y no vuelven a verlo nunca... Por aquellas que destruyen en él toda reminiscencia, lo vacían, lo renuevan y le reservan su mirada muriente y lánguida, su sonrisa quebradiza y su actitud postrera y congelada.

—¡Confiese usted quién cometió el asesinato! —interrumpió el detective, tomando violentamente los hombros de la muchacha y agitándola con brusquedad.

—¡Ah!... Entonces al fin se llevó a cabo el crimen.

I've never been able to see. Many people seek him out. Especially women. His life is a mystery. I've never known why so many people are always coming and going in this house. Some come back. Others are completely forgotten..."

"How did you come to work here...?"

"Reading a HELP WANTED... One that said:

"'Pretty, discreet young lady needed. —Private office. —Good salary. —Tel. 123-12.'

"There was an entire collection of us and, among the most promising candidates, I was the one selected..."

"Do you know his taste in women...?"

"It's multiple and varied... In his secret antechamber, he collects a panoply of gazes and smiles...

"He has a predilection for the dead... Or for those who die on him, leaving behind a sensation, a final, uncontinuable, irrepressible emotion no one else can have, no one else can savor... Or for those who act like they're dying and never see him again... For those women who crush in him all reminiscence, emptying him out, rejuvenating him and reserving for him their languid, dying gaze, their fragile smile and their final, frozen gesture."

"Confess that you know who committed the murder!" interrupted the detective, violently taking the girl by the shoulders and brusquely shaking her.

"Oh...! So the crime has finally been committed."

5

—Él es incapaz de asesinar. Estoy segura que no es culpable...
Sin embargo...

—Sin embargo... ¿qué?...

—Yo presencié los ensayos.

—¿Los ensayos? —preguntó desconcertado el detective.

—Hasta esta oficina en que nos encontramos llegó
un ruido extraño, como de querer abrir una cerradura
sigilosamente.

Voces contradictorias discutían algo que no pude percibir por el tono tan en sordina con que se pronunciaban
las palabras.

Hablaron en secreto, confidencialmente, casi con
caricias...

La dama con quien aclaraba ciertas cosas íntimas, tenía
un aire indiferente. Se notaba en el matiz de las frases un
afán de convencerla, de reanimarla...

Al principio las palabras que articulaban, apenas se
oían, pero ya después se oían menos. Tuve la sensación
de que se iban alejando por la perspectiva intrincada de
las discusiones... Las hacía imperceptibles y las apagaba
su carácter sereno y sistemático, que pone en todos los
momentos una discreción absoluta.

—¿Cómo era la dama con quien él discutía?

—No me fue posible verla, sino a través del velo espeso
que cubría su rostro. Ella, seguramente, desde antes, ya lo

5

"He's incapable of murder. I'm sure he's not guilty... Nevertheless..."

"Nevertheless... what...?"

"I witnessed the rehearsals."

"The rehearsals?" asked the detective, disconcerted.

"A strange noise reached the office where we find ourselves, like someone trying to silently open a lock.

"Contradictory voices discussed something I couldn't discern due to the muted tone in which they pronounced each word.

"They spoke in secret, confidentially, almost with caresses...

"The lady with whom he was negotiating certain intimate themes had an indifferent air. One could note in the shading of his phrases an eagerness to convince her, encourage her...

"The words they articulated could barely be heard at first, but then even less. I had the feeling they were withdrawing due to the intricate perspective of their arguments... It was making them imperceptible, extinguishing their serene, systematic character, which imposed an absolute discretion at all times."

"The lady, what was she like?"

"I couldn't see her except through the heavy veil covering her face. She was surely already expecting him... He arrived alone, surprised by the visit.

esperaba en la habitación... Él llegó solo, asombrado de
la visita.

No supe quién recibió a la dama y no le di importan-
cia a este incidente. En esta casa llena de irregularidades y
amueblada de trucos, todo es posible...

—¿Qué personaje interpretó él durante esa escena?

—El más atractivo. El personaje conquistador e irresistible. Elegante, galante, displicente y distraído. Usaba
actitudes de aventurero romántico. Un traje claro a grandes
cuadros amarillos.

El humo de su cigarrillo ruso prolongaba el vaho
cálido de sus frases.

—¿No observó ningún detalle de la dama?

—No, ninguno. Sólo una palabra que balbuceó con
una voz descolorida.

—¿Con una voz descolorida?

—Sí. Con esa voz descolorida de las mujeres que han
ido destiñendo sus conceptos en las discusiones aburridas.
Tengo la seguridad que esa dama se teñía la voz... No era
sincera al discutir. No se exaltaba. No cambiaba de tono.
Siempre el mismo timbre ficticio...

—¿Qué palabra pronunció?

—No recuerdo. Más bien, no la puedo reconstruir.
Me pareció de un idioma extraño y extravagante.

—¿Por el acento no puede precisarla?

—No. Porque tenía el acento de varios idiomas. Un
poco de alemán, un poco de latín, de griego, de francés,
de inglés, etc.

—¿Esperanto?...

—¿Qué?...

—Prosiga usted.

Pasaron breves instantes, tan inconmensurables como
esos de los sueños. Escuché el hilo de una discusión que

"I don't know who saw her in and I didn't assign the incident any importance. In this house full of irregularities, furnished with tricks, everything is possible..."

"Which character did he play during this scene?"

"The most attractive one. The seductive, irresistible character, elegant, gallant, cavalier and easily distracted. With the look of a romantic adventurer in his light, yellow-checkered suit.

"The smoke of his Russian cigarette prolonged the warm vapor of his phrases."

"You don't remember anything about the woman?"

"No, nothing. Just one word she muttered in a faded voice."

"In a faded voice?"

"Yes. That faded voice of women whose conceptions have been washed out by dull discussions. I'm sure she dyed her voice... She wasn't sincere in her arguments. She didn't shout. She didn't vary her tone. She always had the same fictitious timbre..."

"What was the word?"

"I don't remember. Rather, I can't reconstruct it. It seemed to be in some strange, extravagant language."

"Can't you identify it by the accent?"

"No, because she had the accent of several languages. A little German, a little Latin, Greek, French, English, etc."

"Esperanto...?"

"What...?"

"Go on."

"A few brief instants went by, as incommensurable as those in dreams. I heard the thread of a discussion that seemed directed at someone else due to the violence of the argument."

parecía dirigida a otra persona por la violencia con que se sucedían las argumentaciones.

—¿De qué color era su voz?

—Esa segunda persona, que supongo fue otra mujer, no articuló una sola sílaba. Escuchaba en silencio y resignada... Cesó repentinamente la discusión y él salió hacia este salón, en el que presencié lo más inverosímil.

Con un revólver en la mano, hacía lo posible por parecer exaltado. De pronto se enmascaró de un semblante asesino... Caminó unos cuantos pasos. Retrocedió. Volvió al punto en que se situara antes... Contaba estrictamente los pasos, buscando la mejor orientación del crimen y ensayaba, con verdadero gesto teatral, el ataque y la actitud del asesino elegante.

Iba de un extremo a otro de la habitación, pronunciando en voz baja, palabras para voz alta y exasperante. Desistía de esta manera de asesinar y planeaba una nueva, la rechazaba, ideando otra, luego otra, luego otra...

Así pasó largo tiempo, hasta que, seguramente, descubrió la posición perfecta del criminal, encontrando la actitud certera.

Salió con aire de haber solucionado sus preocupaciones, atravesó el *hall*. Y en la habitación en que lo esperaba su víctima sonó un disparo...

"What was the color of their voice?"

"This other person, whom I assume was another woman, didn't articulate a single syllable. Resigned, she listened in silence... The discussion suddenly ceased and he came into this salon, where I witnessed the strangest thing.

"A revolver in hand, he did all he could to seem enraged. He abruptly put on the mask of a killer... Took a few steps. Retreated. Went back to the point where he was previously situated... He closely counted his steps, seeking the proper orientation for the crime, rehearsing the attacks and attitudes of an elegant killer with true theatricality.

"He went from one end of the room to the other, muttering words meant to be shouted in exasperation. He desisted in one way of murdering and planned another, then rejected it, devising another, then another, then another...

"He spent a long time like this, until he assuredly discovered the perfect criminal position, coming across an infallible attitude.

"He crossed the hall, leaving with the air of having solved his problems. And in the room where his victim was waiting, a shot rang out..."

6

—Es él —murmuró quedamente la muchacha—, despegándose de las manos y de las miradas excrutadoras del detective y desbandando sus pensamientos y sus emociones, mientras el presunto protagonista del crimen, subía las escaleras de la ansiedad.

Tras las primeras pisadas, se escucharon otras que parecían reclutadas por aquellas escaladoras de las situaciones dilucidantes.

Inmediatamente se sucedieron otros pasos y luego otros.

Se tenía la sensación de que entraba uno de esos batallones de las *films*, renovadas constantemente por las mismas comparsas...

Seguido de varias personas sensacionales y austeras, penetró en un salón insospechado para el detective, el mismo individuo que ensayara y planeara el crimen, dirigiendo un rápido saludo. Y sin permitir que se le contestara, empujó y cerró violentamente la puerta secreta de la habitación, dejando al detective y a la muchacha en la tangente de las investigaciones...

Despojándose del sombrero, del abrigo y de la actitud hermética que siempre le había caracterizado y ofreciendo un asiento a cada uno de sus acompañantes, aclaró:

—Mis cómplices son innumerables. Es inútil decir sus nombres y aprehenderlos. No se podría... Unos han salido del círculo y en la órbita en que ha girado mi vida

6

"It's him," the girl whispered discreetly, detaching herself from the detective's grasp and scrutinizing gaze, disbanding her thoughts and emotions as the alleged protagonist of the crime climbed the staircase of anxiety.

After the first footfalls, others could be heard, seemingly recruited by those alpinists of elucidating situations.

There immediately followed others, then others still.

It gave the sensation of an invasion by one of those cinematic battalions that's constantly recycling the same troupe...

Accompanied by several austere, sensational characters, the same individual who may have rehearsed and planned the crime penetrated a salon unsuspected by the detective, offering him a curt greeting. And without allowing him to answer, he violently closed the room's secret door, leaving the girl and the detective on an investigatory tangent...

Shedding the hat, coat and hermetic attitude that had always characterized him and offering a seat to each of his companions, he began his exposition:

"My accomplices are innumerable. It's useless to name and apprehend them. It'd be impossible... Some have left my circle and, in the orbit in which my life has revolved since I met this woman, others have emigrated or deserted my friendship. But they've all contributed to clouding my conduct.

desde que conocí a esta mujer. Otros han emigrado o desertado de mi amistad. Pero todos han contribuido a enturbiar mis procederes.

Los que actualmente intervinieron en el crimen, no es posible citarlos y reunirlos aquí... Son innumerables, inconmensurables...

—Insujetables...

—Que la vida se tome la molestia de irlos desterrando...

Para sintetizar las investigaciones y evitar su captura innecesaria y difícil, me declaro el único culpable, a pesar de que tengo probabilidades de evadirme y pruebas irrefutables de mi inocencia...

—Señores jurados incidentales reunidos aquí en plebiscito supernumerario...

No me interroguéis...

No necesito defensor...

Soy un asesino anónimo...

No soy un criminal...

Mi única defensa es el crimen. Y ni siquiera lo será mañana... Porque no lo consumé del todo...

Cuando tropecé con la mujer irresistible, toda mi fuerza y todo mi anhelo se polarizó en la indiferencia y en la imposibilidad de conquistarla...

Hice de mi persona una serie de personas. Catalogué en mí mismo una envidiable variedad de individuos. Fui el más completo muestrario de hombres, física-moral-intelectual-socialmente, y ninguno de ellos lograba interesarla. Recurrí a todos los precedimientos humanos, artísticos, literarios, científicos, imbéciles, hipócritas, para imbuirle un sentimiento. Celos, triunfos, displicencias, fracasaron ante su mutismo. Hubiera desistido si sus ojos no expresaran, en irregulares momentos, cierta intención

"Those who presently intervened in the crime cannot be subpoenaed... They're innumerable, incommensurable..."

"Insubjectable..."

"May life take the trouble of exiling them...

"To synthesize the investigations and avoid their unnecessary and onerous apprehension, I declare myself to be the only guilty party, even though I have every opportunity to escape and irrefutable proof of my innocence..."

"My dear incidental jurors gathered here in a supernumerary plebiscite...

"Don't interrogate me...

"I don't need an attorney...

"I'm an anonymous murderer...

"I'm not a criminal...

"My only defense is the crime. And even that won't last until morning... For I didn't fully consummate it...

"When I tripped over that irresistible woman, all my strength and all my desires polarized in her indifference, in the impossibility of conquering her...

"I crafted my persona into a series of personas. I cataloged within myself an enviable variety of individuals. I was the most complete sampler of men, physically-morally-intellectually-socially speaking, and none of them managed to interest her. I turned to all human, artistic, literary, scientific, imbecilic, hypocritical preceedings to give it feeling. Jealousies, triumphs, apathies all failed in light of her silence. I would have desisted if her eyes didn't irregularly express a certain intention and a certain desire to find in me the ideal man. I possessed the qualities and beauties of that man, but

y cierto deseo de encontrar en mí el hombre ideal. Yo tenía las cualidades y las bellezas de ese hombre. Pero descontroladas, desorganizadas, dispersas. No faltaba, sino orientarlas, dinamizarlas, encauzarlas.

Inventé, sin eficacia, frases sinceras y convincentes. Frases suspicaces, frases arteras, innobles, mortificantes, joviales y todas naufragaban en su sonrisa impenetrable.

Durante los frecuentes insomnios —los mejores diccionarios— hojeé mis posibilidades de hombre, sin encontrar la palabra que ella esperó tanto tiempo.

En los huecos de silencio que, a veces, me recluían de la obsesión, se arrinconaba esperanzada de escuchar la frase mágica... Se arrellanaba en actitudes fáciles de ensamblar con esa que yo ensayé continuamente y que me dio cierta impersonalidad... Cierto simultaneismo en mi carácter y en mis gestos.

Pasaron intrincados instantes y los dos coincidíamos en buscarnos, en querernos hallar, en cortejarnos, demostrando una férrea reincidencia.

Un día, sin pensar, sin analizar el sentido y la intención, con la más grande de las despreocupaciones y con la seguridad de que no se tomaría en cuenta mi promesa y de que la dejaría inconmovible, por decir algo que cortara el silencio que nos desahuciaba, la dije:

—Por ti, sería capaz de cometer un asesinato...

Saltó hacia mis brazos como si la hubiesen desamarrado, como si hubiesen soltado todas las velas de su ilusionismo. Y, besándome frenética, claudicante, alocada, desbaratada toda ella de su ideología inconquistable, abrió de par en par sus miradas que tenían cierta herrumbre de ensueños...

Una frase cualquiera, pronunciada sin ningún antecedente, sin ninguna tendencia, la exasperó y la acercó a mi

uncontrolled, unorganized, dispersed. All they needed was orientation, dynamization, canalization.

"I fruitlessly invented sincere and convincing phrases. Wary phrases, cunning phrases, ignoble, mortifying, jovial, all shipwrecked on her impenetrable smile.

"During my frequent bouts of insomnia—the finest of dictionaries—I paged through my manly possibilities, unable to find the phrase she had been so long awaiting.

"In the hopes of hearing that magical phrase, she took shelter in the hollows of silence that occasionally sequestered me from obsession… Settling into attitudes easy to assemble with the one I was continuously rehearsing and which gave me a certain impersonality… A certain simultaneism in my character and gestures.

"Intricate instants went by and we coincided in seeking each other out, wanting to find each other, court each other, displaying an iron recidivism.

"One day, without thinking it over, without analyzing meaning and intention, with the greatest unconcern and confidence that my promise would not be considered, that I would leave her unmoved, simply to say something that would cut through the silence that had declared us moribund, I told her:

"'For you, I'm capable of murder…'

"She jumped into my arms as if suddenly unbound, unfurling all the sails of her illusionism. And, kissing me frantically, recantingly, madly, her whole being spoiled of her unconquerable ideology, she opened wide eyes that had a certain fantasy rust…

"A random phrase, uttered without precedent, without direction, exasperated her and drew her into my life forever.

vida para siempre.

Nunca imaginé que esta promesa incidental la conquistara...

Sus miradas, sus gestos, sus caricias, iban subrayando, cada vez con más fuerza, la frase terrible...

Desde entonces no tuve sino un pensamiento. Un pensamiento que obstruccionaba mi cerebración y me guiaba, como una linterna sorda, hacia el crimen.

Intenté comprar la vida de alguien que estuviese desesperado...

Salía en las noches tumultuosas de ideas y de sensaciones incomprensibles, en busca de un asalto, de una discusión que degenerara en insultos y se convirtiera en pistoletazos... En busca de algo que me decidiera a ser criminal...

Los pensamientos pasaban en mi cerebro, como las noches y los días. Con esa alternativa de las noches y los días que dejan esa resolución oscura y decidida, aclarada y desechada con el alba...

Me fue imposible seguir viviendo así. No tuve más salvavidas que el del crimen. Y medité los medios de cometer el más complicado...

De todas las mujeres que me visitaban había una que la exasperó siempre por su belleza, por su gracia, por sus encantos, por su inteligencia.

Cenamos varias veces, bailamos en diferentes ocasiones, íbamos al teatro los tres, con una envidiable compaginación espiritual...

Cuando ella estaba preparada sentimentalmente, voluptuosamente, para presenciar el crimen, cuando presentí que lo contemplaría con un verdadero fervor, tracé los planos del asesinato y lo ensayé como un actor perfecto

"I never imagined this incidental promise would conquer her...

"Her gazes, her gestures, her caresses underlined that terrible phrase with ever more force...

"Since then, I've had but one thought. A thought that obstructed my cerebrations and guided me to the crime like a deaf lantern.

"I tried to buy the life of someone desperate...

"I went out into nights turbulent with ideas and incomprehensible sensations, in search of a robbery, an argument that would degenerate into insults, becoming gunshots... In search of something that would make up my mind to become a criminal...

"Thoughts passed through my head like nights and days. That alternation of nights and days which leaves behind a resolution with the dawn both obscure and determined, revelatory and forsaken...

"It was impossible for me to go on like this. I had no salvation but crime. And I meditated upon the means of committing the most complicated one...

"Of all the women who visited me, there was one who always exasperated her because of her beauty, her grace, her charms, her intelligence.

"We had dinner together several times, danced on different occasions, went to the theater as a trio with an enviable spiritual collation...

"When she was sentimentally, voluptuously ready to witness the crime, when I foresaw that she would contemplate it with true fervor, I sketched out the plans for the murder and rehearsed it like a perfect actor on a perfect stage...

"To grant the spectacle greater solemnity, a special booth was decorated with all the tones of the yellow

en un escenario perfecto...

Se tapizó un gabinete especial con un color "amarillista", un color que diera más solemnidad al espectáculo... se amuebló con un mobiliario sombrío que completara la decoración y contribuyera a hacerlo más sensacional...

En ese gabinete nos reuníamos asiduamente. Durante aquellas frecuentes citas, fui caracterizándome como un verdadero criminal. Como un criminal psicológico que presiente los detalles que van a impresionar más...

Estas reuniones fueron para los tres de una tortura indescriptible...

Hubo momentos en que el crimen parecía irremediable...

Los fui prolongando hasta que se desbordó la inquietud.

Una noche en que tomábamos el té, entre la trivialidad de la charla que provocan todos los tés, creí, totalmente, en la posibilidad de realizarlo. Me iba sintiendo asesino...

Mi *flirt* de criminal las desconcertaba y las fue acercando más y más. Estas escenas me uniformaron de cinismo y una noche. Esa noche de la tragedia, después de haberme colocado en situaciones difíciles, considerando que no se podía prolongar la espectación, decidí consumar el asesinato...

La amiga que me acompaña es la única testigo del crimen.

El maniquí que me librará de la cárcel está inspirado en su belleza. Es mi más grande amiga y lo será siempre...

¡Señores jurados incidentales reunidos aquí en plebiscito supernumerario!

Que este crimen provisional, que puede ser precursor del verdadero, quede en un absoluto silencio...

press... outfitted with somber furniture that would complement the decor and contribute to heightening its sensationalism...

"We assiduously gathered in that booth. During those frequent rendezvous, I began to characterize myself as a true criminal. A psychological criminal who senses which details will best impress...

"These gatherings were an indescribable torture for the three of us...

"There were times the crime seemed irremediable...

"I drew things out until restlessness overflowed its banks.

"At tea one evening, in that conversational frivolity all teas induce, I came to fully believe in the possibility of its execution. I started feeling like a murderer...

"My criminal flirtation disconcerted them and drew them closer and closer. These scenes dressed me in the uniform of cynicism, and one night, the night of the tragedy, after having placed myself in difficult situations and considering that I could no longer prolong the sense of expectation, I decided to consummate the murder...

"The woman who accompanies me was the only witness to the crime.

"The mannequin that will free me from prison was inspired by her beauty. She is my closest friend and always will be...

"My dear incidental jurors gathered here in a supernumerary plebiscite!

"May this provisional crime, which could be the precursor to the true crime, remain cloaked in absolute silence..."

LA SEÑORITA ETCÉTERA

A mis compañeros de cuartillas
en El Universal Ilustrado

SEÑORITA ETCETERA

For my partners in print
at El Universal Ilustrado

1

Llegamos a un pueblo vulgar y desconocido.

Todos los pasajeros habíamos urdido esa fugaz amistad de calceta provisional que se urde durante el ocio de un camino vertiginoso de hierro. Por un accidente inesperado, tuvimos que dejar un momento los vagones y asaltar la primera estación del itinerario. La ciudad estaba a oscuras. Los huelguistas habían soltado un tumulto de sombras y de angustias sobre la turbia ciudad sindicalista.

Caminábamos un poco medrosos y el frío nos hacía más amigos, más íntimos, más sensibles.

Yo compré mi pasaje hasta la capital, pero por un caso de explicable inconsciencia, resolví bajar en la estación que ella abordó. Al fin y al cabo, a mí me era igual... Cualquier ciudad me hubiese acogido con la misma indiferencia. En todas partes hubiera tenido que ser el mismo.

Sin duda, el destino, acostumbrado corregidor de pruebas, se propuso que yo me quedase aquí, precisamente aquí, con ella.

La calle fue pasando bajo nuestros pies, como una proyección cinemática. Era la hora en que todo parece estar en convalecencia. Las cosas se iban quitando sigilosamente su antifaz cloroformizado.

Los mástiles de los barcos empujaban su ansiedad, queriendo descolgar los frutos encendidos más allá de los cielos. De cuando en cuando, la concavidad gigantesca del

1

We came to a vulgar, unknown town.

The passengers had all knitted that provisional stocking of fleeting friendship frequently knitted during the dead time of a queasy iron journey. An unforeseen accident forced us to temporarily abandon the train, storming the first station along the route. The city was in darkness. Strikers had unleashed a riot of shadows and anxiety on the murky syndicalist city.

We walked hesitantly; the cold drew us closer, made us friendlier, more sensitive, even intimate.

I had bought a ticket to the capital, but, understandably impulsive, resolved to get off at the station where I'd seen her board. It was all the same to me in the end... Any city would have received me with the same indifference. I would have had to be the same person anywhere.

Destiny, that inveterate editor, had doubtlessly decided that I would remain here, right here, with her.

The street went by under our feet like an unspooling reel of film. It was that hour when everything appears to convalesce, the chloroform mask slowly, silently falling away from the face of things.

The shipmasts pushed aside their anxiety, eager to harvest the burning fruit beyond the skies. From time to time, strange movements could be seen in the great concavities of overhanging trees, their tightly packed

árbol, movía inusitadamente sus ramajes de bote en bote, desprendiendo el inevitable fruto picado por los pájaros ultracelestes... La inquietud lo levantaba subsilente, como en un juego de *base-ball*.

Ella me contemplaba en silencio. Yo no podía eslabonar ningún pensamiento con mis ideas "empasteladas" por los sacudimientos de la alta marea.

Sentado junto a ella, en medio de la soledad marina y de la calle, me sentía como en mi casa. Disfrutaba de un poco de música, de un poco de calor, de un poco de ella.

Cuando empezó a estilizarse la decoración imaginista, me di cuenta de que había estado alucinado de un sueño.

Era una ciudad del Golfo de México. Acaso yo me encontraba allí por una equivocación en las direcciones de mi bagaje ilusorio.

De todas maneras ya no tenía remedio.

—¿Qué iba a hacer?

Lo de siempre.

Nada.

Me acostumbraría a vivir detrás de una puerta o en el hueco de una ventana. Solo. Aislado. Incomprendido. Tendría que pregonar por unas cuantas miradas o unas cuantas sonrisas, algunas EXTRAS de mi vida inédita.

Como no hablo más que mi propio idioma, nadie podrá comunicarse conmigo.

Tendría que volver a contemplar, confundidas con los programas idiotas que se embobaliconan en las esquinas intelectuales de las ciudades civilizadas, mis sensaciones desbordadas con la tinta dolorosa de la vida.

Para asirme más a la absurda realidad de mi ensueño, volvía a verla de vez en cuando. El azar, interrumpiendo la perspectiva de un viaje arbitrario, nos acercaba sin

branches shedding the inevitable fruit pecked by empyrean birds... And subsilently elevated by restlessness, like during a baseball game.

She studied me in silence. I was unable to make a single thought connect with my ideas jumbled by the convulsions of the tide.

Yet by her side, in the solitude of street and sea, I felt at home. I enjoyed a little bit of music, a little bit of sun, a little bit of her.

When the imaginist scenery became stylized, I realized I had been taken in by a dream.

I was in a city on the Gulf of Mexico. Perhaps I had found myself there due to an error in routing my illusory baggage.

In any case, it was pointless.

"What was I to do?"

The same as always.

Nothing.

I would get used to living behind closed doors and in the bays of windows. Alone, isolated, misunderstood, I would have to advertise for a few glances or smiles, extras in my undiscovered life.

Since I don't speak any language but my own, communication with others was impossible.

Confused with the idiotic propaganda that dazzles the intellectual corners of our civilized cities, I would have to once again examine my feelings overflowing with the painful ink of life.

From time to time I went to see her, clinging still further to the absurd reality of my daydream. Chance, interrupting the prospects of an arbitrary journey, brought us together without introductions, without precedents.

presentaciones, sin antecedentes. Era inevitable y hasta indispensable que siguiésemos juntos. Además, la casi furtiva amistad que enhebramos, me había hecho creer que estaba enamorado de ella.

El sueño comenzaba a desligarme. Sentí cansancio. Su languidescencia doblada sobre mis brazos con la intimidad de un abrigo, se había dormido. Era natural. Seis días de viaje incómodo, la hicieron perder su timidez. No era por nada... El cansancio también la desligaba de todas sus ligaduras sensitivas.

Pensé. Ella podría ser un estorbo para mi vida errátil, para mis precarios recursos. Lo mejor era dejarla ahí, dormida. Huir...

De pronto, me acordé del calendario amarillento de mi niñez sin domingos, del alba atrasada de mi juventud, de mi soledad.

Acaso ella, era ella...

Y me eché a andar yo solo, hacia el lado opuesto de su mirada.

It was inevitable and even indispensable for us to keep it going. Besides, the furtive friendship we threaded even led me to believe I was in love with her.

Sleep began to undo me. I was weary. She drifted off, her languidity folded over my forearm with the intimacy of an overcoat. It was natural. She had lost her shyness after six days of uncomfortable travel. It wasn't for nothing... Her weariness also freed her from all emotional bonds.

I got to thinking. She could be a nuisance for my errant lifestyle, my precarious resources. It would be best to leave her there, asleep. To flee...

Suddenly I remembered the yellowed calendars of my Sundayless childhood, the late dawning of my adolescence, my solitude.

Her, it could only be her...

And I got up and walked alone toward the opposite end of her gaze.

2

1, 2, 3, 4, 5, 6, 7, 8, 9, 10, 11, 12, 13, 14, 15, 16, 17, 18, 19, 20, 21, 22, 23, 24, 25, 26...

—¿Un reloj?

No. No es posible.

Imposible.

Mis ojos se fueron quitando, poco a poco, la goma del amodorramiento de las noches palingenésicas, del insomnio producido por el ajetreo mental, que se va extendiendo en un cansancio de corriente apagada, por las fibras de nuestro equilibrio sensorial.

Una campana seguía clavando en la beatitud de la ciudad, su humilde inconsecuencia.

Un sentimiento impreciso me agarraba del cuello.

Con la temblante seguridad de que a una leve insinuación de sus movimientos hubiera desandado la idea de alejarme, me paraba a cada momento.

Su recuerdo se enrollaba en mi espíritu.

Su voz naufragaba en el sonambulismo de la hora, como las voces muertas de los teléfonos.

Inútil oponerse. Yo estaba condenado a olvidar todas las cosas. A despegarme de ellas, con una facilidad torturante.

Tal vez había perdido lo único que hace bella la rotación de nuestras elipses...

Ella se quedó, allá, muy lejos, descendiendo del paracaídas de su ensueño. Yo, arrastrando su recuerdo, me dirigí al café.

2

1, 2, 3, 4, 5, 6, 7, 8, 9, 10, 11, 12, 13, 14, 15, 16, 17, 18, 19, 20, 21, 22, 23, 24, 25, 26...

"A clock?"

No. It's not possible.

Impossible.

My eyes slowly rid themselves of the sleep of palin-genetic nights, the insomnia brought on by the mental tumult extending through the fibers of my senses with all the weariness of an open circuit.

A bell kept hammering away in the midst of the city's beatitude, its humble inconsequence.

An imprecise feeling grabbed me by the neck.

I had to constantly check myself, possessed by the trembling certainty that just a mild insinuation of her movements would undo the idea of leaving her behind.

Her memory coiled in my spirit.

Her voice foundered on the somnambulism of the hour, like the dead voices of telephones.

It was useless to resist. I was condemned to forget everything. To unburden myself with a torturous ease.

Perhaps I had lost the only thing that could grace a rotation along the ellipse...

She was still far off, parachuting down from the day-dream of her. Dragging her memory behind me, I headed to the café.

El café llegó a ser mi otro yo. Todos los días, todas las noches, después de la cotidiana vagamundez de mi trayectoria, aburrido de encontrar las mismas siluetas escrutadoras en las callejuelas, de contemplar la estúpida fachada de las casas y la sonrisa boba de las ventanas, me refugiaba en el café.

Casi me iba acostumbrando a su vida inmoble. Me divagaba con sus frases estereotipadas en la pared, con sus caras parroquianas, con su aislamiento de las calles estentóreas y vociferadoras. Hay algunos cafés tan aproximados a la vida, que dan la sensación de que uno cena, bebe, fuma, ríe, en medio de la calle, con los transeúntes impertinentes, estropeadores... En donde es muy posible que, distraídamente, nos tomen del brazo y nos sigan contando la misma aventura a lo largo de la calle...

Los espejos multiplicaban simultáneamente, con una realidad irrealizable de prestidigitación, las imágenes "rimmeladas" de mi catálogo descuadernado.

Cuando la vi por primera vez, estaba en un rincón oscuro de la habitación de su timidez, con una actitud de silla olvidada, empolvada, de silla que todavía no ha ocupado nadie...

Sus ojos tenían una impávida inocencia de la vida. Parecíase a esas mesas de los cafés, embrolladas de números, de cuentas, de monigotes, de intimidades de los parroquianos asiduos.

Sin duda estaba allí por necesidad... Viéndola, auscultándola, vivía retrospectivamente.

Sus miradas, sus sonrisas, sus palabras, me envolvían en la bruma de los instantes vividos en un vagón ahumado de imposibles.

The café had become my double. Every night and every day, after my habitual wanderings left me bored of finding the same searching silhouettes in the alleyways, of contemplating the stupid façades of houses and windows like idiotic grins, I took refuge in the café.

I almost got used to its stagnant life. I lost myself in the clichés on its walls, the faces of its regulars, its isolation from the stentorian, vociferous streets. There are some cafés that approximate life so well they give the feeling of dining, drinking, smoking, laughing in the middle of the street, surrounded by abusive, impertinent pedestrians… Where they might lead us distractedly by the arm, telling us of some adventure all the way down the road…

The mirrors simultaneously multiplied the mascaraed images of my unbound writings with the unrealizable reality of a conjuring trick.

The first time I saw her, she was in a dark corner of the bedroom of her shyness, with the posture of a forgotten chair covered in dust, a chair nobody has ever sat in…

Her eyes shone with a fearless innocence of life. She resembled one of those café tables cluttered with numbers, bills, doodles, intimacies left behind by assiduous customers.

There was no doubt she was there out of need… Watching her, auscultating her, I lived retrospectively.

Her glances, her smiles, her words enveloped me in the haze of living moments in a railcar choking with the smoke of impossibilities.

In my imagination, she no longer existed on her own, she was no longer merely herself; she was fused, confused with that other her I rediscovered in the corner of a café.

Since then, I have been unable to live my nights and days separately.

En mi imaginación ya no existía solamente ella, no era solamente ella; se fundía, se confundía con esta otra ella que me encontraba de nuevo en el rincón de un café.

Desde entonces, ya no pude vivir los días y las noches separadamente.

Mi ocio se había quedado, como el de los demás parroquianos, pegado a la pared.

Cuando ella servía, indiferente a todos los intrusos que ensordecían el ambiente de humo y de gritos, me alejaba un poco entristecido, sin pensar en su embrujamiento.

Una noche entré al café con la intención de decirla muchas cosas, de continuar una conversación que nunca habíamos tenido, pero que yo consideraba interrumpida.

Al acercarse, me miró de tal manera, que sentí encenderse el recuerdo de la mirada de ella.

Balbuceó no sé qué palabras, como en secreto, y la hice una promesa:

—Nos veríamos siempre.

My leisure time, like that of the other diners, remained indecisively stuck to the wall.

As she waited tables, indifferent to the intruders who deafened the atmosphere with shouts and smoke, I walked away with a broken heart, without thinking of the spell she was under.

I came to the café one evening intending to tell her many things, to continue a conversation we had never begun but that I felt had been interrupted.

As I approached, the way she looked at me inflamed the memory of her gaze.

She stammered something unintelligible, like a secret, and I made her a promise:

"I'll be seeing you, always."

3

El balanceo premeditado por las irregularidades de la vía, sacudiendo las sombras del vagón, desintegraba un sueño de doscientos kilómetros.

Los *porters* nos habían repartido en las celdas del *pullman*, con una intransigencia insoportable.

De cuando en cuando, la fuga del paisaje al carbón, emborronada por la acelerada carrera del tren, hilvanaba a mi vida interrumpida por las estaciones.

Los pasajeros eran los mismos de siempre.

Al bajar, los claxón de los automóviles olfateando la traza de los viajeros, se acercaban con zalemas zigzagueantes de reconocimiento, coreando su insistencia

LIBRE

El otoño comenzaba a recoger las primeras hojas volantes que repartía el viento.

Yo me sentía con esa profunda nostalgia que se va acumulando en las estaciones solitarias, recordadas por unas cuantas luces mortecinas, alegradas o entristecidas por los pitazos de los trenes.

Mi espíritu se ensombrecía como esos carros desorillados de rieles mohosos, en los escapes de las vías.

Yo no era más que un carro en donde todo se había ido, un carro olvidado, con sus miradas perdidas paralelamente, a lo largo del paisaje.

3

The rocking of the car, premeditated by the irregularities of the track, rattled its shadows and broke apart two hundred kilometers of sleep.

The porters had distributed us throughout the compartments of the Pullman with a terrible intransigence.

Landscape smeared by the acceleration of the train occasionally leaked through the smoke and threaded itself into my life interrupted by stations.

The passengers were the same as always.

Upon arrival, klaxons picked up the scent of travelers and approached in fawning zigzagging reconnaissance, chanting their insistence:

ON DUTY

Autumn began to collect the first handbills distributed by the wind.

I felt the profound nostalgia that accumulates at solitary railway stations, remembered only for their dying lights, consoled or saddened by the whistling of the locomotives.

My spirit darkened, like a train left behind on an overgrown railway siding.

I was nothing but a railcar that had been emptied of everything, forgotten, its sights concurrently lost in the landscape.

Agobiado, ahumado de tantas saudades, empecé a recorrer las emociones desconocidas que atardecían en la ciudad.

Bajo el azoramiento de las calles desveladas de anuncios luminosos, me dejaba estrujar por sus turistas, sus mujeres elegantes, sus *snobs* de la moda y del sistemático vagar por las aceras desenfrenadas.

El parpadeo de mi semáforo columbró, a lo lejos su silueta confundida de vela que se desprende y se va a pegar a los mástiles atmosféricos, cuando un viento agita la epidermis del mar.

No tenía la seguridad de que fuese ella, pero su figura descolgaba de la galería de recuerdos, se estatizaba en la penumbra de un daguerrotipo.

Caminé tras ella con la paradoja de que era ella, de que su voz submarina volvería a colorear la esponja de mi corazón que se llenara continuamente de remembranzas de ella.

Su andar ligero impulsaba mi astenia. Casi me arrepentía de haberla dejado instintivamente a la orilla del mar o en la habitación oscura de un café.

El contacto inesperado con la multitud, hizo balbucientes mis ideas, mientras ella se alejaba con mayor rapidez de mi memoria.

Cuando casi me decidía a confesarla mis presentimientos, se perdió al través del cristal de la vitrina de un almacén.

La contemplé imaginariamente.

Quería retener sus contornos, sus miradas, sus sonrisas. Adivinaba sus movimientos para desasirse, para librarse de mí.

Overcome, my spirit clouded by saudades, I set out to navigate the unknown emotions fading in the city's dying light.

Falling under the frenzied spell of insomniac streets blazing with neon lights, I let myself be crushed by their tourists, elegant women, fashion snobs and flaneurs in systematic wanderings down insatiable sidewalks.

Off in the distance, the flickering of my semaphore glimpsed her confused silhouette of a sail cutting loose and wrapping around atmospheric masts as the wind agitates the epidermis of the sea.

I wasn't sure it was her, but her portrait was taken down from my gallery of engrams, expropriated in the penumbra of a daguerreotype.

I walked after her aware of the paradox that it was her, that her submarine voice would once again shade my poriferous heart, which had been constantly soaking in recollections of her.

Her brisk pace left me asthenic. I almost regretted having instinctively left her by the seaside or in the dark chamber of a café.

An unexpected brush with the multitude made my brain stutter as she ever more rapidly distanced herself from my memory.

Just as I had almost resolved to confess my presentiments, she disappeared behind a display window.

I contemplated her in my mind's eye.

I wanted to hold on to her curves, her eyes, her smiles. I divined her attempts to unmoor herself, free herself from me.

Se quedaba para siempre entre perfumes, embalsamada de alucinaciones, de esperanzas. Se quedaba ahí, eternizada. Se esfumaba...

No me quedaría de ella, sino la sensación de un retrato cubista. Una pierna a la moda con medias de seda, ruborizada de espejos... La otra en actitud hinojosa... La insinceridad de sus guantes crema... Su mirada impasible... Su ropa interior melancólica... Su recuerdo con pliegues... Se disasociaba en la vitrina de un almacén lujoso, infranqueable...

She lingered there forever among the perfumes, embalmed in hallucinations, hopes. There she remained, immortalized. And vanished...

I had nothing left of her but the sensation of a cubist portrait. A fashionable leg in a silk stocking, blushing in the mirror... The other bending at the knee... The insincerity of her cream gloves... Her impassive gaze... Her melancholy lingerie... Her pleated memory... She disassociated in the window of a luxury department store, unassailable...

4

Todos los días, a la misma hora, con la irrevocable necesidad de tener que utilizar algunas horas de mi involuntaria pero arraigada vagancia, tomaba el tranvía.

Los tranvías subrayaban todos los días, todas las tardes, de ocho a doce y media y de tres a cinco y media, la carta de recomendación de mi amigo. Cambié de traje, de humor, de maneras. Mi rebeldía casi se iba acostumbrando a esas existencias de calcomanía de las oficinas.

Por la influencia del ambiente, tuve que agregar a los recortes literarios de mi vida, sellos oficiales, ideas mecanográficas, frases traslúcidas de papel carbón, imprecisiones de goma de borrar, pensamientos aguzados uniformemente con *shapeners*...

El motivo de mi llegada a la metrópoli, la causa de haber abandonado tantas cosas, se iba borrando, hundiendo. La realidad de que podría llegar a los ascensores intelectuales, me impulsaron a hacer innumerables arbitrariedades imborrables que agitaban mi espíritu.

Había salido de una oficina insignificante para entrar a una oficina importante. No había hecho más que lo mismo...

4

Every day at the same time, out of an irrevocable need to use up a couple hours of my involuntary yet unwavering vagrancy, I took the trolley.

Every morning and every afternoon, from eight to twelve-thirty and from three to five-thirty, the trolley underlined my friend's letter of recommendation. I changed my clothes, my mood, my manners. My rebelliousness nearly even got used to those transferware realities of offices.

Under this environmental influence, I had to supplement my life's literary clippings with official seals, typewritten ideas, phrases revealed on carbon paper, erased imprecisions, thoughts uniformly honed by pencil sharpeners…

The reason I had come to the metropolis, the cause for which I had given up so much, began to vanish, disappearing beneath the waves. The reality that I could ascend the intellectual elevators encouraged me to commit innumerable, indelible injustices that troubled my spirit.

Mi vida fue tomando un aspecto de piso encerado. Diariamente arrancaba a mi disciplina de calendario, la hoja numerada del fastidio del día.

Una vez que robé al horario de la oficina, con la intención de tomar el tranvía a una hora alegre, diferente, entre el abigarramiento apretado de mujeres, ella subía empujada por la precisión.

Sentí impulsos de no tomar el mismo tranvía, de dejarla pasar inadvertidamente, de que no me recordara la figura que me obsesionaba.

Después abordé premeditadamente el tranvía a la misma hora en que ella lo tomaba.

Sentado, silencioso, contemplándola, encerrado en su indiferencia, me divagaba con la conversación babelesca de los anuncios hipnotizadores en el interior del carro.

Ella se balanceaba armoniosamente de las agarraderas...

En mi interior, repetía las mismas palabras para ofrecerla el lugar que me reservara la casualidad. Se lo ofrecía con los ojos, con el pensamiento, con actitudes imaginales, pero ella se iba alejando poco a poco...

Muchas veces la esperé con un vacío interior.

Mis sentimientos se desbordaban por las ventanillas, por el *troley*, que iba dejando desgarramientos luminosos de su fibra sensitiva...

El esmalte de sus cabellos cortos, en espirales acariciantes, su voluptuosa transparencia al andar, la comisura de su sonrisa, me exacerbaban.

Bajo su mirada fulgurante de

I left an insignificant office to work at an important office. I did nothing but more of the same...

My life took on the aspect of a freshly-waxed floor. Each morning, my calendrical discipline tore into the day's numbered nuisance.

Once, when I embezzled from the schedule with the intention of taking the trolley at another, happier hour, I found her in a kaleidoscopic crush of women, pushed aboard by precision.

I felt an urge to wait for the next one, to let her pass by unawares, to not remind myself of someone who had so obsessed me.

But I later deliberately boarded at the exact same time.

Sitting silently, considering her, enclosed in her indifference, I got lost in the babble of hypnotic ads plastered along the inside of the car.

She swung harmoniously from the handrails...

In my head, I kept repeating the same phrase offering her the seat that chance had reserved for me. I offered it with my eyes, my thoughts, my imaginary gestures, yet she slowly backed away...

I often waited for her with an inner emptiness.

My feelings spilled out the window, leaving behind a luminous trail of frayed nerves...

I was aggravated by the gloss of her cropped hair curled up in caressing spirals, her voluptuous transparency as she walked, the corner of her smile.

Beneath her stunning gaze of

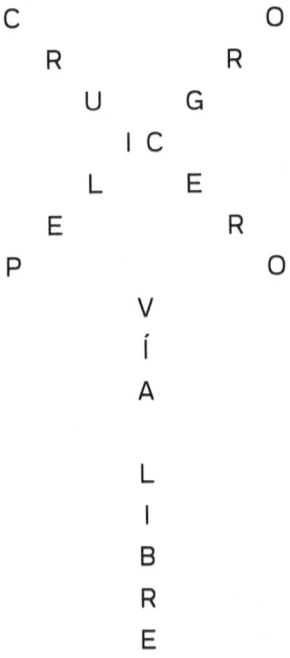

```
        C                   O
          R               R
            U       G
              I C
                L   E
              E           R
        P                   O
                V
                í
                A

                L
                I
                B
                R
                E
```

sus senos y mi corazón se que-
daron temblando, exhaustos, con ese temblor incesante
del motor desconectado repentinamente de un anhelo de
más allá…

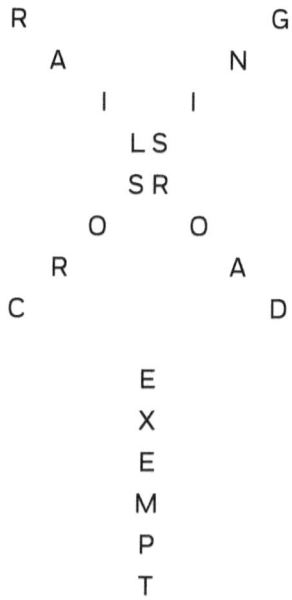

her breasts and my heart were left trembling, exhausted, in the incessant tremor of a motor suddenly disconnected from a longing from the beyond...

5

Ya tenía mucho tiempo de vivir en la ciudad y no conocía nada de la ciudad. Apenas si conjeturaba algo del cuarto que ocupara en el hotel.

Al principio tuve la intención de pagar, en una casa de huéspedes, un mes de vida mediocre. Las súbitas impresiones me llenaron de penumbra el cerebro y no pude hacerlo. Yo nunca he tenido sentido común.

Tomé un cuarto en el hotel más lujoso. Un cuarto que jamás utilicé, porque pasaba los días y las noches en lugares inusitados.

No me sentí vivir en aquel hotel, sino cuando ella penetró, con sus pasos medidos, en el ascensor.

Subíamos lentamente y tan irreales como ese humo que enferma la garganta de las chimeneas...

La vida casi mecánica de las ciudades modernas, me iba transformando. Mi voluntad ductilizada giraba en cualquier sentido. Me acostumbraba a no tener las facultades de caminar conscientemente. Encerrado en un coche, me perdía en el sonambulismo de las calles.

Yo era un reflector de revés que prolongaba las visiones exteriores hacia las concavidades desconocidas de mi sensibilidad. Las ideas se explayaban convergentes hacia todas las cosas.

Me volvía mecánico.

5

I had been living in the city for some time and yet I knew nothing of the city. I barely had half a hypothesis regarding the hotel room I inhabited.

At first, my plan was to pay for one mediocre month in a guest house, but sudden impressions filled my head with shadows and I couldn't do it. I've never had common sense.

I took a room in the most luxurious hotel. A room I never once used, as I spent my nights and days in stranger places.

I didn't feel alive in that hotel until she penetrated the elevator with her measured steps.

We ascended slowly, as irreal as the smoke that sickens the throats of chimneys...

I was being transformed by the nearly mechanical life of the modern city. My pliable will bent in every direction. I got used to not having the ability to consciously walk. Enclosed in a car, I lost myself in the somnambulism of the streets.

I was an inverse reflector prolonging all my visions of the outside world toward the unknown concavities of my consciousness. Ideas expounded upon themselves, converging on everything.

I became mechanical.

Me conducían las observaciones puestas en cada uno de los objetos que usaba.

Cuando el ascensor concluyera de desalojarnos, encontrándome de pronto frente a ella, la observé detenidamente, me estupefacto de que también se había mecanizado. La vida eléctrica de hotel, la transformaba.

Era, en realidad, ella, pero era una mujer automática. Sus pasos armoniosos, cronométricos de *fox-trots*, se alejaban de mí, sin la sensación de distancia. Su risa se vertía como si en su interior se desenrollara una cuerda dúctil de plata. Sus miradas se proyectaban con una fijeza incandescente.

Sus movimientos eran a líneas rectas, sus palabras las resucitaba una delicada aguja de fonógrafo. Sus senos temblorosos de "amperes"...

Ya en el diván de su cuarto, comenzamos a recordar las mismas cosas de siempre.

Nos escuchábamos ambos desde lejos. Nuestros receptores interpretaban por contacto hertziano, lo que no pudo precisar el repiqueteo del labio.

Me sentí asido a sus manos, pegado a sus nervios, con una aferración de polos contrarios.

Las insinuaciones de sus ojos eran insostenibles; yo los asordinaba con una pantalla opalescente.

Cuando ella desató su instalación sensitiva y sacudió la mía impasible, nos quedamos como una estancia a oscuras, después de haberse quemado los conmutadores de espasmos eléctricos...

Ella había llegado a ser un APARTMENT cualquiera, como esos de los hoteles, con servicio *cold and hot* y calefacción sentimental para las noches de invierno...

I relied on the notes placed on each of the objects I used.

Suddenly finding ourselves face to face when the elevator finished evicting us, I observed her carefully, astonished to see that she, too, had been mechanized. The electric life of the hotel had transformed her.

It was really her, but she was an automaton. Her harmonious steps keeping time for a foxtrot, she moved away from me but felt no further distant. Laughter poured from her mouth as if a silver cord was unspooling inside of her. She projected her gaze with an incandescent resolve.

She moved in straight lines, her words brought to life by a delicate phonograph needle. Her breasts quivering with amperes...

Once we settled on her divan, we began to recall the usual things.

We listened to each other from a distance. Our receivers interpreted through Hertzian contact what couldn't be understood through the percussion of our lips.

I felt anchored to her hands and bound to her nerves in the grip of opposite poles.

The insinuations of her eyes were unbearable; I muted them with an opalescent screen.

When she discharged her emotional system and disrupted my impassive counterpart, we were left like a darkened room, its switches burnt out by electrical spasms...

She had become an anonymous apartment, like those in hotels, with hot and cold service lines and sentimental heating for winter nights...

6

Mi sombra se alargaba en los jardines con una pesadumbre de persiana apagada. Desencantado de una tristeza retrospectiva, su remembranza cosmopolita de suntuosidades de *hall*, con música de piano automático, sus miradas, sus sonrisas de antesala, me hacían daño...

Aunque ella había adivinado la oscuridad de mis primeros pasos en la ciudad, aunque ella me sacó con su mirar "eclatante" de ojo de automóvil —de la callejuela apagada de barrio bajo en que transitaba... —Ella no podía ser ella...

Me había tatuado, quemando hondamente su silueta en el fondo de mi corazón, extenuado de tantas emociones.

Indudablemente yo era un "papalote" de la vida. Cuando me encontraba más allá de sus manos, casi inmóvil, o vibrando con la misma inquietud de su ocio infantil, me atraía o me alejaba inevitablemente.

Ya era más que un vagabundo de las calles y de la vida, era un vagabundo del pensamiento, no podía estandarizar las células de mi cerebro exaltado.

¡Era posible que el destino, hojeándome diariamente, no encontrase lo que encontraba en todos los demás!...

Ella me vio tendido, en un banco de un parque, con las manos metidas en los bolsillos de mi interioridad, de mis recuerdos.

Había seguido las tendencias de las mujeres actuales.

6

My shadow lengthened in the garden with all the sorrow of drawn blinds. Disenchanted with a retrospective sadness, I was wounded by cosmopolitan memories of magnificent halls echoing with player piano music, of her eyes, her foyer smiles...

Though she had discerned the darkness of my first steps in the city, though her dazzling automobile eye had rescued me from a lifeless slum alleyway... It couldn't be her...

She had tattooed me, profoundly branding her silhouette on the depths of a heart exhausted from so many emotions.

I was undoubtedly nothing but a kite in life. Whenever I found myself out of her reach, whether almost perfectly still or restlessly vibrating in time with her childish idleness, she inevitably drew me close or cut me loose.

I had become more than just a vagabond in the streets, in life; I was a vagabond of thought, unable to regulate the cells of my fanatical brain.

It's possible that destiny, looking me over each day, wouldn't find what it had found in everyone else...!

She saw me sprawled out on a park bench, my hands shoved deep into the pockets of my introspection, my memories.

She followed the trends of contemporary women.

Era feminista. En una peluquería elegante, reuníase todos los días con sus "compañeras". Su voz tenía el ruido telefónico del feminismo...

Era sindicalista. Sus movimientos, sus ideas, sus caricias estaban sindicalizadas...

Cuando le hablé de mis idealidades peregrinas, se rió sin coquetería.

Azuzaba la necesidad de que las mujeres se revelaran, se rebelaran...

Quería convencerme de que nuestra vida es vulgar, como la de cualquiera, de que no éramos más que unos visionarios, de que era indispensable hacer una revolución espiritual. Sanear las mentalidades de tanto romanticismo morboso...

Yo escuchaba sus palabras con la ecléctica indiferencia que tengo para la charla de las peluquerías...

Los espejos no retrataban sus mohines frívolos... Feministas.

Mientras ella recortaba algo de mi vida ilusoria y me prodigaba sus caricias de *Fleurs d'Amour*, yo sufría la tiranía de sus abrazos que me atenaceaban con la simplicidad de las toallas amortajadoras de clientes.

Sus modales, sus palabras, me sugerían ese terrible agasajo de los *office-boys* de las peluquerías, que me hacían abandonar los establecimientos, medroso de que intentaran arreglar mi modo de ser... De acepillarme las ideas, de quitarme algo... De ponerme algo...

Sin embargo, cuando salí, yo veía naufragar en el agua de los espejos sindicalistas, sus miradas de *Un Jour Viendra*...

She was a feminist. Every day, she met up with her "sisters" in an elegant beauty parlor. Her voice rang with the telephonic noise of feminism...

She was a syndicalist. Her movements, her ideas, her caresses had all been unionized...

When I spoke to her of my transient ideals, she laughed dryly.

She incited women to reveal themselves, to rebel...

She tried to convince me that our lives were vulgar, like those of all the rest, that we were nothing more than visionaries, that we had to undertake a spiritual revolution. To cure our mentalities of all that sickly romanticism...

I listened to her words with the eclectic indifference I reserve for barbershop talk...

Mirrors wouldn't reflect her frivolous grimaces... Feminists!

Tearing a page from my illusory life and lavishing me with *Fleurs d'Amour* caresses, I suffered the tyranny of her embrace, which tormented me with all the simplicity of a funerary towel shrouding a client's face.

Her words, her manners suggested those terrible receptions of office boys in barbershops that always made me flee such establishments, afraid they would try to spruce up my way of being... Brush away my thoughts, lop something off... Or apply something...

Yet when I left, I saw her glances of *Un Jour Viendra* sink beneath the waters of the syndicalist mirrors...

7

Cada vez que su recuerdo desovillaba mis letargos, tenía que engañarme para no buscar la claridad de su sombra.

Sus absurdidades, tan naturales, desmantelaron la ráfaga de ilusión que navegaba en sus pupilas.

No podía desarraigarme de su influencia. Sin embargo, de cuando en cuando, lograba olvidarla momentáneamente, mientras herían mis saudades las voces de las demás mujeres.

A pesar de que su transformación había sido sistemática, yo estaba seguro de que, en el fondo, ella seguía pensando con los pensamientos míos...

Interiormente, la llevaba iluminada con el mismo fervor con que ella me había sacado de mi existencia oscura.

Divagando por las calles desteñidas de lluvia, con la tenacidad de eternizar su inencontrable figura, me refugiaba, intermitentemente, bajo las pestañas de las marquesinas.

Estaba agobiado de mí, de sensaciones sentimentales. Por más que intentaba pensar en la vida dinámica, una casa astrosa, un farol insomne, un papelero bajo la lluvia, un mendigo incrustado en un rincón, hacíanme desalojar remordimientos incomprendidos, nostalgias compasivas que me deterioraban...

En la puerta de un cine, el timbre saqueaba a los transeúntes. Me detuve un instante para explicarme su realidad.

7

Whenever her memory unraveled my lethargy, I had to deceive myself to keep from seeking out the clarity of her shadow.

Her absurdities, which came so naturally, undid the torrent of illusion I navigated in her pupils.

I couldn't uproot myself from her influence, though I managed to momentarily forget her whenever the voices of other women wounded my saudades.

Though her transformation had been truly systematic, I was sure that, deep down, she was still thinking my thoughts...

Inwardly, I kept her image illuminated with the same fervor with which she had drawn me out of my obscure existence.

Rambling through streets discolored by rain, stubbornly immortalizing her untraceable figure, I found intermittent refuge under the eyelashes of the awnings.

I was overwhelmed by myself, by my sentimental sensations. I tried to focus on the dynamic life, yet the sight of a dilapidated house, an insomniac streetlight, a newspaper vendor in the rain, a beggar lodged in a corner was enough to upset all my misunderstood regrets, the tender nostalgia that wore me down...

The insignia at the entrance to the cinema despoiled the pedestrians. I stopped for a moment, trying to understand this reality.

Sus pasos apenas si rozaban el silencio aglomerado numéricamente en las butacas.

Su silueta se había desteñido. El ambiente descolorido en que vivía le daba ese aspecto.

Toda ella se había quedado en mi memoria, con una opalescente claridad de celuloide...

Transitaba jardines agitados por un viento eléctrico, con florescencias inanimadas, humedecidas por una lluvia de surtidor...

Sus miradas estaban hechas de *dissolvesout*, su voz tenía siempre el mismo tono modulado con ritmos de silencio articulado.

Todas las noches, como en un sueño, yo desenrollaba mi ilusión cinemática...

Her footsteps barely chafed against the silence numerically accumulated in the seating.

Her silhouette had lost its color, an aspect lent by the achromatic environment she inhabited.

Her whole being had been captured in my memory with the opalescent clarity of celluloid...

Withstanding electric wind and irrigated rain, she crossed gardens glowing with an inanimate fluorescence...

Her gaze was made of dissolves and her voice always had the same tone, modulated by rhythms of articulated silence.

Each night, as in a dream, I unwound my cinematic illusion...

8

Mis evocaciones estaban agujereadas de sus miradas de puntos suspensivos... Sentado al borde del crepúsculo, las repasaba sin pensar.

Había peregrinado mucho para encontrar la mujer que una tarde me despertó hacia un sueño. Y hasta ahora se me revelaba.

Presentía sus miradas, etc. ... sus sonrisas, etc. ... sus caricias, etc. ... Estaba formada de todas ellas...

Compleja de simplicidad, clara de imprecisa, inviolable de tanta violabilidad.

8

My reminiscences were perforated by her elliptical gaze... Sitting on the threshold of twilight, I skimmed them unthinkingly.

I had come far to find the woman who one afternoon woke me up to a dream, revealing herself to me until now.

I sensed her gazes, etc.... her smiles, etc.... her caresses, etc.... All of them aspects of her...

A complex simplicity, an ambiguous clarity, an inviolable violability.

Arqueles Vela

Arqueles Vela (1899-1977) is a cult author if there ever was one: though he is cited as writing the first piece of avant-garde prose in Latin America ("Señorita Etcetera," 1922) and forming part of Mexico's Stridentist movement, which became a password for later generations of literary rebels, there is much about him we don't know— not even his country of birth. Some sources mention Guatemala, others Mexico.

As bureau chief of *El Universal Ilustrado*, he championed Mariano Azuela, the great novelist of the Mexican Revolution, as well as up-and-coming writers such as Gilberto Owen. He took an irreverent approach to the magazine: one article, for example, was illustrated entirely with photos of women's hands, even though this had nothing to do with the text. He also used his editorial position to defend the early poetry of Manuel Maples Arce, the controversial founder of Stridentism, which led Maples Arce to recruit him for the movement.

His early writings would contain few signs of the revolutionary impact of his breakthrough story, "Señorita Etcetera," when it was published in *El Universal Ilustrado* the following year. Later included in his first collection, published in 1926, this story introduced experimental prose techniques to Mexican literature at a time when much European modernist literature had not yet been published in Latin America. When Maples Arce moved Stridentism's base to Veracruz to take advantage of the governor's offer to patronize the movement, Vela stayed behind in Mexico City; he later went to Spain as

a foreign correspondent and spent several years traveling around Europe. His first novel, *The Non-Transferable Man*, built on the innovations of his early stories but went unpublished for 50 years due to the collapse of the Stridentist movement.

Upon his return to Mexico in the early 1930s, Vela began working for the Public Education Secretariat, promoting the arts at night schools for workers. He would resume writing fiction in the forties, albeit in a somewhat less experimental key. These later works have largely fallen into neglect and his reputation rests on his writings of the 1920s—above all, "Nobody's Café" and "Señorita Etcetera." He died in Mexico City in 1977.

Julianna Neuhouser

Julianna Neuhouser is an American-Mexican translator and writer who specializes in radical politics and modern and contemporary art. Her previous translations have included Osvaldo Bayer and Sergio González Rodríguez, while her writings have been published in outlets such as *Gatopardo*, *ZonaDocs*, *Malvestida*, *Trans Safety Network*, and *Revista Común*.

Veka Duncan

Veka Duncan is a Mexican art historian specializing in Mexican art, architecture, urban history and cultural press of the 19th and 20th centuries. She worked as a researcher for Mexico City's *El Universal*, where she developed books for its centennial, and she has collaborated in over 20 exhibitions in Mexico and abroad as researcher, curator and translator. Currently, she hosts a television show about Mexico City history and is a columnist for *El Cultural* and *Opinión 51*. She is the author of *Cara o Cruz: Lázaro Cárdenas* (Taurus, 2019) and *Luis y Caro vs. los fantasmas de la ciudada* (Alfaguara Infantil, 2023).